Stargazing

by

Kathy L. Salt

I0621539

2018

Stargazing © 2018 Kathy L. Salt
Triplicity Publishing, LLC

ISBN-13: 978-0999737071
ISBN-10: 0999737074

This is a work of fiction. Names, characters, places, and incidents are the product of the author's imagination and are used fictitiously. Any resemblance to actual persons, living or dead, business establishments, events of any kind, or locales is entirely coincidental.
Printed in the United States of America

First Edition – 2018
Cover Design: Triplicity Publishing, LLC
Interior Design: Triplicity Publishing, LLC
Editor: Haley White - Triplicity Publishing, LLC

A big thank you to Marco and Kim who I can always rely on for comments and read-throughs. I want to thank my little sister Evelina for lending me her recipe for cashew tacos. I would also like to thank my editor Haley White who gave me loads of encouragement and feedback. Last, I want to thank Sanna and Sara who brighten up all my days.

To Lud -
Here's to another eleven years.

CHAPTER ONE

Star found herself tied to a chair. Handcuffs cut into the skin of her wrists; the leopard fur on the inside of the cuffs she had seen before being blindfolded must have been quite worn. Star didn't care. She couldn't focus on anything but the tantalizing sound of her co-star laughing somewhere to the left of her. Star knew what she looked like, she'd worked with her before, but not being able to see her, not knowing when Ana was going to touch her was *torture.* Ana was whispering something, but Star didn't listen to the words. Instead, she listened to the slight humming from the filming equipment. The words weren't for her anyway. They were for *them.* Their audience. Present and future.

The hair on her arms stood up when Ana came closer. The air around Star filled with the scent of sweet vanilla and warmth, and her heart sped up. A cold hand cupped her breast and fingers squeezed her nipple. Hard. Star gasped and struggled in her restraint. Her mouth fell open but no sound came out.

Ana laughed again and released her touch. Her treatment of Star was almost cruel, but it was what people paid for. They wanted to see Star restrained, made submissive. It was the number one request, according to her agent. That and strap-on scenes.

Ana ran her hands through Star's short hair and grabbed a hold of it at the nape of her neck, forcing her head backwards. Star groaned and her mouth fell open again. She was dying for Ana to kiss her. To give her something. Any sign of tenderness to make the ordeal worth it. It didn't matter how.

The wetness between her legs was cooling and goose bumps stood on all four of her limbs. It wasn't usually this cold, was it? She moved her shoulders, wanting to stretch.

"You're stuck." Ana straddled her legs and put her hands on Star's shoulders. "Poor baby." She nipped at Star's bottom lip. "You just wait. I'm going to rock... your... world." In one fluid movement she moved from Star's lap, sat on the floor, and pushed her legs apart. Star held her breath as Ana leaned in and started to feast.

*

Lissa stared open-mouthed at the GIF that played over and over on the screen in front of her. Heat flushed to her face, igniting her skin. Her heart started pounding in her chest. *Stupid internet, it should really come with a warning label.* She swallowed once. Twice. *Just scroll past it.* Of course she was going to scroll past it. She wasn't going to sit there and stare at—

"Liss?"

With a small gasp, Lissa closed her screen just before her sister Dea stuck her head through the doorway. She kept her hand on the lid, terrified that Dea would ask to check something or even come closer when Lissa still hadn't scrolled past the GIF of two women doing... *well.*

"What is it?" She sounded a bit more annoyed than she felt. "Sorry. I was just in the middle of... something." She shook her head and tried to smile casually but knew that she was still blushing. She hoped that Dea wouldn't notice. Or at least wouldn't comment on it.

"You work too much." Dea made a face, ever the caring older sister. "I was wondering if you wanted lunch. I brought some caesar salad, I thought—" She fell silent. "Are you okay? You look… ill."

"I'm fine," she hurried to say. "I'll be right downstairs. Just give me a minute." She sighed with relief when Dea just nodded and disappeared from her doorway.

Lissa opened her laptop again and stared at the GIF with wide eyes. She didn't even know what it was about the two women—no, just the one on top—that was so captivating to her. There was something tantalizing about her. Something primal. She had short dark brown hair, and her body was—

"Lissa! I'm hungry!" Dea called out.

"Start without me." Lissa wasn't ready to stop looking yet.

The women were kissing now, but the black-haired one turned her face away from the camera, opening her mouth as if gasping for air. At the same time, the brunette on top started biting at her neck with fervor. Neither ceased their other movement either. The one on top was strapped and it was clear what they were doing.

More than anything, Lissa couldn't stop staring at the brunette woman's face. Her face was rather round, but not in a soft or delicate way, just round. Her hair was short, cut close to her skull, and her olive skin created a nice contrast to the much darker skin of the woman underneath. Her mouth was curled into a possessive grin, but her eyes were gentle as she looked down upon the woman at her mercy. At a later frame, her grin became a surprised laugh as if she couldn't believe the pleasure she was feeling.

That laugh sent a surprised jolt all the way to Lissa's clit. She took a deep breath and made the conscious choice to click 'x' up on the right and closed her laptop.

Now go and play nice with Dea, she told herself, *then maybe after work today you go out or something. Can't stay cooped up inside like this. It's driving you insane. Or at least overly horny.*

She closed her laptop and headed downstairs.

"There you are." Dea had opened her food container and dug in. "I didn't know that inviting you here meant you would work all the time."

"I thought you invited me here to water your plants and look out for your home while you were away."

"Yes." Dea smiled widely, showing off a piece of lettuce stuck between her front teeth. "But now I'm back and I need my office for studying." She was joking. Both of them knew it. They didn't live in the same town, so any time they spent together was worth gold. "Nah, I'm just joking. You know I want you to stay."

"I do." Lissa looked at her fondly, fighting the urge to tug on Dea's blue hair. "But I've got a party to go to. I'll be back in a few weeks though." She stopped fighting the urge and pulled Dea into a quick hug, curling a lock of blue around her finger like she had done since they were small. She didn't want to leave. She had been getting increasingly jaded with work lately. She would have much rather lived with Dea in their late parents' house close to the campus than in the city center. In her tiny, tiny studio apartment.

"I know you have to work. I just miss you," Dea talked into her shoulder.

"I miss you too." *Maybe I should just quit my job,* Lissa thought. *Move here. Surely there is something else I can do?* "At least we will have the whole weekend next time. That I promise."

*

Star cracked her shoulders; the muscles in her back and butt were aching. What she really needed was a hot bath, not to go to a party, but there was no way she was staying in her barren apartment all weekend. Just the thought killed her.

So that was why, in spite of sore muscles and a sense of agitation in her head, Friday afternoon found her in her bedroom. She had been told they were probably staying over from Friday to Saturday, so she made sure to pack extra underwear and a T-shirt to sleep in. She was about to close her bag when her phone rang.

"Star."

"Finally. I tried calling earlier but your phone was turned off. Or something." Deirdre's dry tone filled Star's ear. Her oldest friend. Their friendship was so old that Star couldn't remember why they were friends in the first place. Deirdre didn't approve of any part of Star's life.

"I was working."

Deirdre sighed. "Of course you were."

I don't want to get into this again. Star threw another pair of socks into her bag, which was stupid since this was California and she would wear sandals the entire weekend.

"Never mind." The pursing of Deirdre's lips was almost audible. "I just wanted to make sure that you're coming to the party tonight."

"Oh." Star dropped her toothbrush and let it fall into the bag while straightening her back. "I already have plans. I already promised Macie and Carla to go with them to this beach house over the weekend with a couple of other women."

"Who the hell are Macie and Carla?"

"Just some new friends of mine. They're cool," she said.

"Star." Deirdre sounded annoyed. Maybe she had hoped that Star would drop everything and come running? Because of a party? Then she really didn't know Star at all. "It's for Malena. She's back."

Star sucked in a breath. *Malena was back?* When? Why?

"I can tell from your silence you didn't know."

Star stopped moving, sat down on the bed, and put her head in her hands. Shame filled her belly, creating a stone of discomfort. She hadn't called Malena the whole time her friend had been away.

"I'll be there." Her mouth was dry, her eyes strangely wet. "Just text me the details." Star didn't wait for Deirdre to answer. She hung up.

CHAPTER TWO

Lissa stood on the upstairs balcony looking out over the glittering sea. She stared out at the horizon. There were worse locations to work. She tore herself away from the beautiful view and walked inside the kitchen, ready to tell her people what to do. Her boss, Yolanda Powell, was infamous for hiring incompetent but cheap people, and Lissa knew from previous experience that she needed to take charge.

She grimaced when the two teenage workers made two carrots perform an obscene act.

"People are going to arrive soon, and I'd like the food to be ready for when they do." Lissa grabbed the cheese and started grating it, hoping that she wouldn't get cheese on her black shirt.

"I hope you'll be ready on time," the client, Deirdre Herland, said as she came into the kitchen. She walked with urgent steps, stopping to pick up a red bell pepper. She looked down at the phone in her hand, sighed, and then looked at Lissa and raised one of her eyebrows. "What is this? Tacos?"

"No, Ms. Herland. It's a taco salad. Ms. Lucio requested it."

"And you didn't call to confirm with me?" As soon as the question was uttered, Lissa suspected she had made a mistake. "Even though I'm paying?"

Lissa's eyes widened. It happened, but it wasn't often she met a client this rude. The cogs started spinning in her head, and she quickly tried to think of something to say.

"I apologize." She didn't stop the movement of her fingers and continued to grate the cheese. "I was under the impression you're co-paying."

Deirdre opened her mouth, looking like she wanted to argue. Her phone beeped.

"Well. I'm here. As instructed." A woman entered. She went right up to Deirdre. "And you tricked me, the party isn't for another hour. I could have showed up at Macie's and—"

"I'm going to stop you right there." Deirdre put her phone down. "You would have been late or not even shown up." Her features softened a bit and she pulled the shorter woman into a hug. "Hi, Star. Nice to see you again." Star hugged her back.

She was of average height, probably just a tad shorter than Lissa herself, with brown, spikey hair that suited her. There was something in her easy smile that was so familiar, Lissa had to have seen her somewhere before. Maybe from…

"Ouch!" A sharp pain shot from the tips of her fingers and down her hand. She looked down and saw a drop of blood seeping out of a tiny cut just next to her nail. She removed her finger before any got onto the cheese and quickly moved the grater too. "Damn it." She felt her face heat up and she looked up at her client in terror. *Fuck.* Ms. Herland was already upset with her and this wouldn't help.

"Here." Star had quickly let go of the embrace and come to her aid.

Lissa was handed a paper towel that she pressed against her finger while looking up at Star. She had definitely seen her before. Suddenly, realization hit her and heat flooded her face so quickly she felt dizzy. The hair was too short, and she was wearing too many clothes, but yes, Star was indeed familiar.

*

Star regarded the woman carefully. Her face was crimson and her eyes were the size of saucers. At first Star was worried that the cut was deeper than she had first thought, but when the woman kept staring at her, Star couldn't help but grin. It didn't happen often—least of all by women—but it was always a little bit of an ego boost when she was recognized.

She took a step back to give her some space.

"Do you have any band-aids?" She turned toward Deirdre, but to Star's surprise, it was the woman who had been cut that answered.

"Probably in the bathroom. That's usually where band-aids are kept."

The woman's eyes were unfocused as she cradled her injured finger. Star almost felt sorry for her.

"Come on." She took a hold of her wrist. "Let's go find some."

"No, I—" She started but Star interrupted her.

"You're not going to bleed all over the food. Come on." She was cute. The fact that she was clearly recognizing her from her job also made Star want to stay in her vicinity for a little bit longer.

"You... you don't have to," the woman stuttered. "I can go by myself."

Star said nothing as they exited the kitchen and walked down the hallway. When she hoped they were out of earshot, she glanced back at her.

"I'm Star, by the way."

"Lissa."

"Nice to meet you, Lissa. I feel kind of guilty."

"Guilty?" Lissa looked at her with surprised eyes.

"Apparently you recognized me from somewhere." Star almost couldn't keep herself from laughing when Lissa turned red again. "Don't panic. I won't mention it to anyone."

They finally found the bathroom and Star ushered Lissa inside, seating her down on the toilet while she looked inside the mirror cabinet for band-aids.

"I... I'm so embarrassed." Apparently Lissa could speak when Star had her back turned. "This is so not professional."

"Don't be embarrassed, ah, here it is." Star finally found a box. "I'm not. Why should I be embarrassed about something I'm good at?"

"I don't know."

"Here." Star turned around and held out a band-aid. "Can you put it on yourself?"

"Of course I can." Lissa took it from her and wrapped it around her finger. "Thank you."

"Any time." Star sat down on the rim of the bathtub in front of her. "So let's start over. I'm Star, best friend of the bitch of a client you have."

She held out her hand, but Lissa didn't take it.

"My hands are cheesy." Lissa smiled coyly. If she had disliked Star's choice of words, she didn't show. "I'm Lissa, the party planner who is currently screwing things up."

Lissa's face was pleasant to look at: small nose, high cheekbones covered with freckles, full lips and pale brown eyes. Light brown hair. Star grinned and opened her mouth. The words were on the tip of her tongue, ready to be said. A pick-up. A suggestion. Maybe just a compliment. She shook her head internally. *This is Malena's welcome home party.* It wasn't the time or place to hit on someone. And not somebody who was currently on the job.

She was about to get up again when Lissa spoke.

"I don't usually watch things like *that*." She looked down at her lap. "I was on social media. It was a GIF."

Star frowned, she didn't know what Lissa meant.

"I didn't know what I did was so repulsive that you need to give me an excuse for why you saw it." She couldn't keep the annoyance out of her voice. *Sigh. I hate hypocrites.* Judgmental types.

Lissa looked up again and their eyes met.

"No! No it wasn't repulsive." Her smile was shy. "Far from repulsive, I…" Her smile went through Star and warmed her all over. "It was… beautiful. You have a nice tattoo." She only had one tattoo, and it ran from her waist, down her hip, and on to the inside of her thigh.

Star smiled, but it was a careful smile. She put her hands in her pockets and stood up. There was nothing for her to get there, and she wanted to join her friends now. "Thanks."

"Let's go back." Lissa stood up too. "I need to get back to work."

"Do you want me to grate it for you?" Star didn't mind. "Not offering out of the kindness of my heart. I just don't want blood on my food."

"I don't think it would be appropriate for you to help out. But if it makes you feel better, I will go downstairs and rearrange the tables before returning to the kitchen. To make sure the blood flow stops." They exited the bathroom.

Lissa gave her one last smile.

"Stay clear of sharp objects," Star called as she disappeared hurriedly around the corner, but she was laughing. Nervously as it may have been, it was still a laugh. And Star liked making women laugh.

Star smiled to herself when she headed downstairs. The beach house where the party was being held was rather small, she just had to walk down the stairs; the living room ended facing the beach with big glass sliding doors. They were open and on the other side, Lissa was pulling a table across the patio. Deirdre was nowhere to be found.

"Need help?" Star hurried forward and grabbed the end of one of the tables. "We'll lift together. One. Two. Three."

"Thanks," Lissa said when they had moved the table to the other side.

"Don't sweat it." Star wiped the sweat off her forehead. It was so hot outside. "Shouldn't you have people helping you do this?"

"Yes." Lissa took out a box of plastic cups and placed them in piles on the table. "There must have been some mix-up at the office. All I got were two teenagers, only one with waitressing experience. The same mix-up as at every party." The last words were mumbled under her breath. "I should get up and check so that they don't mess up in the kitchen."

"I think they already did." Star scratched the back of her neck as she looked straight at Lissa. "It smelled slightly burnt in the stairway."

Lissa sighed and pinched the bridge of her nose.

"Okay, I'll have to check. I cannot, will not, serve burnt food."

Who is this girl? Star felt impressed with Lissa's energy: one-part determination, one-part frustration. She got the feeling that if anybody could turn this around, she could.

"Come on." Their gazes met. "Let's go and check on the food."

As they walked into the house and up the stairs again, Star was grateful that she had come early.

*

So, she's not just sexy. Lissa thought as she wiped the sweat off her brow. *She's also helpful and considerate. Even to staff.* She shivered as sparks shot down her spine, brought on by the simple touch of their arms meeting briefly. *Get a grip, Lissa.* She couldn't look at Star. Every time she did, she started thinking about all she had seen Star do. The possessive look in her eyes when she looked at the woman underneath her. The way the veins in her hands popped when she grabbed the thighs, arms, or waist of the other woman. The look on her face when she came. And she couldn't afford to be distracted. Not while trying to pull off the most disastrous party of the century.

Lissa shook her head again. She needed to get a grip. Maybe as the hours went by, she would eventually forget about Star and who—what—she was.

Oh, crap. She hadn't even reached the top of the stairs yet, and the erosive smell of burnt mince was already reaching her. Her heart started an angry dance and she tried to breathe calmly. She needed to keep cool to contain the situation. Even if one of her idiot employees had destroyed what they were going to serve the guests.

"Hey, are you gonna be okay?" Star grabbed her arm, stopping her.

Lissa turned around, looked down at Star's hand, holding her in place.

Star let go.

"I'll talk to Deirdre," Star said. "She won't give you trouble. Or yell at you."

Lissa laughed mirthlessly.

"Well, I have my pride as well." She sighed. "Come on." She didn't know why she assumed Star would go with her. But they went into the kitchen together.

She found the source of the stench in a serving tray on the kitchen island. She stared, horrified, at the black and burnt mess.

"What did you do?"

"What?" One of the workers took a step back and stared at her. She hated the look in his eyes. Like a deer caught in the headlight.

Lissa couldn't say anything, she just stared.

The other one, the girl, came over to look at the plate.

"Can't we serve it anyway? We can call it 'blackened.'"

Lissa wanted to slap her own forehead.

"No. No, no." She talked slowly while shaking her head. "No, we can't. Let's just double up on the vegetables and—"

"I'd eat it." The man—or boy—grabbed a spoon.

"If you must." Lissa folded her arms in front of her chest. Her brain was running 200 miles a second. *I need to fix this somehow.* "We're not putting it out there. You can have it as a midnight snack, whatever. Just don't let anyone else see it."

"What do you suggest we do then?" The girl tapped her foot on the ground.

"Already told you." Lissa sighed. "But you're right, we do need something meaty for the tacos." She wrinkled her nose and surveyed what they had.

"Do you have any nuts?" Star appeared in the doorway behind her.

"Cashews." Lissa nodded. "But the taste doesn't really go, does it?" She clicked her tongue, tasting the idea in her head like she usually did when thinking about menu options.

"No, but crushed with some spices, soy sauce, lemon juice, and garlic, it tastes almost like mince. Very taco-esque. Perfect for the salad."

Lissa looked at her. Disbelief and cautious relief flooded her mind.

"Can you make it?" It didn't matter that Star was a guest anymore.

"Sure." Star laughed. "I'm not doing it to be nice though, I'm just really in the mood for some cashew tacos." She fixed her gaze on the girl and boy in the kitchen. "Bring me what I need."

*

"This is really good." Star wiped her hand on a napkin and smiled at Lissa's admission. While she had been crushing the nuts, Lissa had removed her business suit and changed into more casual attire. To blend in with the guests better, Star guessed.

She was now wearing a white top and orange shorts, and she had also let her hair down to fall over her shoulders in waves. *She's pretty. Too bad she's on the job and not a guest.* If things had been different, she would have liked to pull Lissa into a corner and get to know her a bit better.

"Hey." Lissa put her hand on Star's upper arm. Her touch was very light. "Thank you so much. I would like to tell you that this has never happened before, but that would be a lie." She let go of Star's arm, folding her own across her chest. Her forehead wrinkled. "Your friend would have done better hiring someone else." She bit her lip. "Not because of me, honestly, but because there are better agencies out there. Trust me."

"So why do you work for them?" Star wanted to touch her tense shoulder. Calm her down.

"I don't know." Lissa sighed. "Habit, mostly." Their gazes met, and Lissa's features changed. They turned soft and she smiled coyly, her face turning crimson. "Why? Do you always like your job?"

Star chuckled and was about to answer when Deirdre entered the kitchen.

"People are arriving, so I hope everything is done." She threw a dismissive look at Lissa and turned to Star.

"Come on, Malena is here."

Lissa had gotten a tray and was starting to gather glasses on it. *She's not going to serve too, is she?* Star made sure to gaze angrily at the two teenagers who were standing all the way over in the other corner, chatting instead of working. *Poor Lissa.* Star wanted to offer to help, but it really wasn't appropriate. Not to mention that Malena was there.

She headed downstairs with Deirdre, not caring about anything or anyone else. All she could see was Malena, standing in the doorway, looking like she never left. She was Star's best friend, her home.

Time seemed to slow as Star walked up to her. All she could see was Malena's smile, her eyes. She didn't hear anything else or see anything else.

"I didn't know you were coming back home."

Tears gathered in Malena's eyes, she opened her arms and pulled Star into an embrace that smelled of novelty cherry perfume and something Star didn't recognize. It didn't matter. Malena *felt* the same and that was what was most important.

"I missed you," she whispered.

"Hey, don't forget about me." Deirdre was suddenly there, pushing her way into their hug. In the embrace, Deirdre seemed to relax too. Shed her armor a bit.

Malena laughed and pressed a kiss to Deirdre's shaved scalp.

"I wouldn't dream of it." She was their glue. The sweetest part of them. And she was finally, finally home.

CHAPTER THREE

When the sun had set, Lissa escaped the party, the serving, and the stress. She couldn't believe that, despite her worries, everything had worked out. Including the food. All thanks to Star. If she hadn't been there to fix the food, Lissa didn't know what she would have done.

She sighed as she walked barefoot along the beach. The sand was warm under her feet even though the sun had already set, and the air tasted sweet on her tongue. A few people were in the water, jumping and laughing in the black and lazy waves.

"What are you doing out here?" Star must have been swimming earlier. Her hair was wet, and all she was wearing were her pants and a bikini top.

A thrill went through Lissa as she struggled to not look directly at the abs she knew were staring her in the face.

"I'm just enjoying the scenery," she said. "Your friends already paid me, but I'm finding it hard to leave." She didn't think she needed to explain why. The warm blanket of the starry sky did it for her.

Star just smiled and came to stand next to her.

"I'm happy everything worked out for you."

"Yes." Lissa held her gaze calmly. "I'm sorry about before."

Star chuckled and shook her head gently.

"Don't worry. It's not like it hasn't happened before. Women who notice me and then freak out, I mean."

A breeze rustled Lissa's curls.

"Really?" Her eyes went wide.

"No." Star laughed again. "I'm not often recognized at all, and if I am it's because I'm moving in circles where… it's more mainstream."

"You must…" Lissa's face suddenly turned completely red. "Uh, never mind."

"What?" Star took a step forward. "What it is?"

Lissa averted her gaze as she laughed, trying to gather her thoughts. She looked down at Star's hand, holding a plastic cup by her side. Her hands looked strong, wrapped around the cup. Lissa tried to pretend like she didn't know how those hands looked wrapped around a woman's hips or fisted in dark curls.

"Have you always wanted to be a party planner?" Star had apparently run out of patience waiting for Lissa to say something.

"I do enjoy it at times, but I originally wanted to be a secretary." She felt herself blushing at the confession.

"A secretary?" Star produced a surprised laugh.

"I like organizing. Writing lists. Executing plans. Having a calendar and writing down dates. Logistics." Lissa shrugged. "Apparently being a secretary wasn't a good enough goal. I floated around at college, enjoying the studying experience more than the actual knowledge." She looked up at the sky. "Gosh, I sound pathetic, don't I?"

"Pfft." Star made a dismissive gesture. "You know why I got my current job? My ex told me that I slept around so much that I might as well get paid for it. That's pretty pathetic too."

"I helped my roommates throw a party," Lissa hurried to say. "One of the attendees asked me to help plan hers. She was going to pay me. It just kind of escalated from there. Once you get into a routine, it's hard to look elsewhere." Lissa was indeed ashamed of how lax she had been while studying, with nothing interesting her, but she had a job that she liked in theory and the pay was okay. One day she would find something else, but today was not that day. "It feels like it's the only thing I know how to do."

"That's cool." Star nodded. "Come on, let's sit down."

They sat down on the beach. The sand was soft underneath their legs.

"Do you—" Lissa bit her lip, a bit too hard. She soothed the sting with her tongue. "Do you like what you do?"

Star leaned forward, resting her elbows on her knees. Her smile was friendly, almost a bit coy.

"Yeah. I mean…" She chuckled awkwardly. "Yeah, I do. But I feel like I'm getting too old for it."

"Really? You don't look so old, eh, I mean…" *I mean you look good.* Lissa tried to not seem too eager to hear Star's answer.

"I'm not *old;* I'm twenty-nine, but in this business that's practically middle-aged. And as much as I love sex, I really must find something better to do with my life. Something that doesn't take so much from me."

Lissa pondered that for a while. Star certainly looked fresh enough.

"Is your name really Star?" She had to know. "Or is it like your screen name or something?"

"No." She shook her head calmly. "My mom was a hippie. It's my legal name. My film name is Tara."

"Star is better than Tara." Lissa laughed. "Sorry, I just want to ask you a million questions."

"You can, you know." Star's face was open. Earnest. And her eyes were beautiful.

"No." Lissa shook her head. "I should get home, I'm staying at a bed-and-breakfast just a couple of blocks over."

"You could stay here, you know." Star bumped their shoulders together. "There are many bedrooms."

"Thanks for the offer." Lissa smiled. "But I don't think it would be appropriate." She was smiling, but she felt sad inside. Meeting Star was a fluke. Already a memory. *Oh, remember that time that I met...* The thought made Lissa feel a bit melancholic.

"You know." Star's voice turned an octave lower. "If you want to watch more than just a GIF, I could link you to one of my favorite videos."

"That's not necessary." Lissa hated how polite and neutral her answer sounded. As if Star had offered her a seat on the subway.

"Your loss." She chuckled.

"Fine." Lissa turned to look at her. She didn't want to seem boring, and she didn't like the knowing look in Star's face. "Send me the link." *I double-dare you.* Part of her didn't think that Star wouldn't.

Star laughed.

"Okay, but not because I'm nice and shit, only because I think you need it." Lissa sucked in air through her teeth. *How dare she?* She didn't know whether to laugh or feel offended.

"Do you have a card with your email address on it? With your job I figured you would have one."

"Yes." Lissa snapped, immediately feeling guilty about the harshness of her tone. Star was just teasing her. "I do have one," she said in a gentler tone. She reached into her bag. "Here."

CHAPTER FOUR

Star yawned and stretched her arms. Her bag had been left in the kitchen when they had arrived and now she went to search for it. She wanted her toothbrush and clean underwear to sleep in.

Star grinned as she went into an empty bathroom. She recalled the hours before when she had seen recognition in Lissa's eyes. Sometimes it was funny to be recognized, perhaps by a seemingly boring, straight housewife. Sometimes it was downright uncomfortable, like when a man gave her a knowing look. But once in a while she was recognized by someone that made her own heart beat faster.

Lissa was adorably uptight, with a sweet smile and beautiful brown eyes. The idea that she had watched Star, that she had *liked* what she had seen; just the thought of it made Star warm inside. And she was still impressed with how Lissa had handled the situation with the idiot workers and the burnt mince. Star couldn't believe she had stepped in and helped, it wasn't in her nature to be that helpful.

When she had finished brushing her teeth and washed her face, she went into one of the bedrooms and was met by Malena lying across the bed, wearing absolutely nothing.

*

When Lissa's phone beeped, her heart started beating fast, and her fingers trembled when she unlocked it and navigated to her inbox. *I can't believe she sent it, how arrogant, why wo*— Lissa's heart sank when she saw that it was only an email from her latest client.

"You're actually disappointed?" She asked herself out loud. "Idiot."

Her phone beeped again.

Mouth dry, fingers trembling, heart thumping, Lissa opened her inbox again.

Star Ciel
01:45
 Here you go.

The actual message was empty, save for an internet link. Lissa hurried to click it, but not before grabbing her headphones. *Just in case.* She wasn't going to watch it. Of course not. *But curiosity isn't bad, is it?*

'Tara and Emily' it said underneath a small video box showing Star's back with the intricate art work of tattoos. There was a play button and a minute counter next to it. *17:34.*

Lissa's heart was now beating loud enough for her to hear it. Her whole body vibrated with tension, she wasn't sure if it was nerves or arousal. The moisture at the juncture of her thighs however, seemed clear on which it was that her body was feeling.

She clicked it. What did she have to lose?

It started with two women making out and quickly jumped scenes. It seemed like a shorter clip from a longer movie, but Lissa didn't think about that. She stared at the screen, mouth open, her breath coming out in short bursts.

She had seen sex on screen before, of course. But fake sex. Acted sex. Apart from that one GIF with Star, she had

24

never seen anything like this before. She couldn't believe that was what she was seeing. That what she was watching was real.

It started with Star and the other woman making out. Star—Tara—was wearing a pair of baggy green pants and a tight black top that looked amazing on her. It would have been easy for Lissa to imagine herself in the other woman's position, to believe that it was her that Star was kissing. But the woman that Star was with was shaped all wrong. She was too tall, and her hair was too fair. She was also more full-figured than Lissa was, with her tiny, perky breasts and slim hips. Maybe Star preferred a curvier woman?

A thrill went through her when Star tilted her head back and produced a rather feminine moan when 'Emily' kissed and licked down her throat. It was so strange knowing that that's what Star sounded like. The very real woman she had met just hours before.

The women on the screen continued to kiss and touch each other while 'Emily's' hand hurried down to open the fly of Star's pants. The laugh that Star provided was different than the friendly chuckles that Lissa had heard in the day. This laugh was knowing, cocky. She leaned back and just watched 'Emily' open her pants and pull down the zipper. Her smirk was lazy, and she brought up one of her hands and fisted 'Emily's' hair.

"Want to taste me?" It was her voice, but in the same time it wasn't. 'Tara's' voice was smoother, more seductive than Star's usual friendly tone. She grabbed a fist of 'Emily's' fair hair and pulled Emily's mouth to where she wanted it.

'Emily' must have been really uncomfortable, but she didn't seem to care. She was moving her head with fervor, and within a few moments she turned to be on her back.

Tara—Star—shed her pants and then straddled Emily's face, without so much as a warning. She had both hands in Emily's hair and started riding Emily's face, holding fistfuls of her hair.

The camera zoomed in on Star's beautifully expressive face. Her eyes were closed, but her mouth was open, pleasure was playing over her features.

Lissa squirmed, increasingly uncomfortable. She also wanted to know what Star tasted like, and how it felt to be in the place of 'Emily.' Having Star pull on her hair that way. Lissa was wet and she knew it. Wet and swollen and painfully empty. She didn't even have words to name the want she was feeling.

Suddenly, the scene changed again and 'Emily' was on her back, Star half-lying on top of her, fingers deep inside of her. Thrusting hard. 'Emily' was looking at her like she couldn't believe what was happening. Star leaned forward and their lips met again. There was something hard about Star's movements, but the kisses looked almost gentle.

Lissa was sweating, and her hand had started to draw round circles around her belly button. It felt like every nerve ending was on fire, and the simple movement caused so many more feelings than it should have. Lissa wasn't feeling jealous, she was feeling curious.

The clip ended suddenly, without any resolution. Without any warning. Lissa was literally throbbing now and she tried to calm her racing heart. She wanted more. She wanted to watch more. Something else with Star. She just wanted to know *more.*

She watched the clip one more time, which didn't satisfy her one bit, except she cranked up the sound in her earphones and listened intently to every sigh, every moan, every little sound that Star produced. She found the sounds more arousing than anything else.

Afterwards, she closed the window and turned off her laptop. She flopped down on her bed, unsure of what to do now. She couldn't sleep. She was just too wired up. She turned to her belly and, with her eyes shut tight, reached between her legs.

CHAPTER FIVE

It was a few weeks later. Lissa stood at the bar in a small pub called *The Crying Nightingale* watching the band playing in the corner. Her newest client—Mrs. Sheilds—wanted the band that was playing, and Lissa had been instructed by her boss to check them out. She had put on a little black dress, earrings, and make-up, ready to blend in with the crowd. What she hadn't expected was there to be no crowd. There were about twenty people there and that was it. It made Lissa feel a bit anxious. She preferred a crowd to blend in with.

She grabbed one of the stools and sat down, her feet dangling a bit. She found, to her annoyance, that her chair tilted and she grabbed at the counter to stop herself from falling.

"Maybe you should work for a company that makes bar stools for small people." There was no question who that voiced belonged to.

"What are you talking about?" Lissa grinned. "I'm pretty sure you're shorter than me."

"Perhaps." Star said. "But we're not talking about me right now, we're talking about you." She turned to the bartender. "Can I have a beer, please? And whatever the lady is having."

Lissa felt her cheeks heat.

"A lemon drop, please."

"A lemon drop? You crack me up sometimes." Star bumped their shoulders together.

"So what are you doing here?" Star continued. Her tone was giddy, sounding a little bit tipsy. "Cruising?"

If Lissa had a drink in her mouth she would have spat it out.

"No!" She laughed nervously. "I'm working, actually." Her nervousness dissipated with each breath. When staring into Star's face, there was no way to still be nervous. There was something so soothing about her.

"Ugh, no!" Star bumped her again. "Are you serious? Do you ever take a weekend off?"

"No. I mean yes. I mean sometimes." Lissa nodded a thanks to the bartender who brought her her drink. "My job is a job that usually falls on weekends though. Most weeks I have Tuesdays and Wednesdays off. Sometimes Mondays. Sundays." *Often I work though.* Lissa didn't need the time off; she wouldn't know what to do with it.

"You look nice." She changed the subject. Lissa hoped that Star couldn't see her blushing in the dim light of the club, but happiness spread through her chest. She hadn't meant to say it out loud. Star did look amazing and regular in the same time, in baggy jeans and a tight top that somehow accentuated her rather nicely muscled biceps.

"Thanks." Star looked down and focused on her drink. "You don't look so bad yourself."

Lissa didn't know what to answer to that, so she took a sip of her drink and didn't answer. Even though there were things she wanted to know about Star and things she wanted to say, there were things to learn in silence too. The way she breathed. The way she looked while relaxed. The way her hands looked curled around her glass. *Seriously, Lissa, stop looking at her hands, this is weird.*

"There you are." A blonde, tall woman that Lissa recognized from the previous week came and put her arm around Star's neck.

Lissa pursed her lips, her heart fluttered nervously. Annoyance filled her body. They had been having such a good time and then this woman just came and ruined everything. It was an unfair thought, and Lissa felt the guilt right away, but it was as if she couldn't help it.

"So who is this?" The woman—Lissa couldn't remember her name—leaned on the other side of Star and looked straight at Lissa.

*

"This is Lissa." Star made the conscious choice to answer instead of Lissa.

"Nice to meet you." Lissa reached out with her hand, but Malena hugged her. Star's and Lissa's gazes met over her shoulder. Lissa looked surprised, but happy, and Star smiled. Malena had always had a knack for making people feel comfortable.

She let go of Lissa after squeezing her shoulders one more time and turned to the bar. "Drinks, please."

Lissa laughed. "You don't think you need to be a bit more specific?"

"Of course not." Malena winked at her. She had come around to the other side, so Lissa was between them. She looked up and down Lissa's body from behind, and licked her lips. She looked at Star and then pointedly at Lissa's form, nodding greedily.

Star knew what she meant and shook her head violently. They were not going to initiate a threesome with Lissa. That was just *not* happening.

Malena pouted but smiled widely and came around Lissa again, throwing her arm casually around Star's neck. She leaned her head on Star's shoulder. Usually such a move invoked feelings of familiarity, friendship, sometimes lust. This time, under Lissa's gaze, it made Star uncomfortable. She didn't know why, but the idea that Lissa thought that she and Malena were together... that Star wasn't *single*... Star didn't like that one bit. Malena and Star weren't together. Well, not really.

If Lissa thought anything of it, she didn't show. She just smiled lightly and then turned to the bartender and ordered a drink. The quirky smile and sparkle in her eye were gone though.

Star tried to focus on Malena instead. Her best friend.

"This was the friend whose party you organized last weekend. Her welcome back party. She was gone..." Star thought for a moment. "How long were you gone?"

"Two years." Malena shrugged. "I almost didn't think I wanted to come back."

"Where have you been?" Lissa asked. She had received her drink now, a yellow thing with a green umbrella stuck in her glass. She sipped at it through a straw while waiting for Malena to answer. It pulled Star's attention to her pretty pink lips.

"Portugal." Malena's hand came up and played when the neckline of Star's shirt. Lissa's eyes followed her hand. "I was looking for my roots."

"Cool." Lissa leaned forward, but Star could have sworn her eyes were still following Malena's hand. "My dad was from Portugal, actually. But I've never been."

"Oh, it's beautiful. You should go. And so—" Star felt Malena's mouth come closer to her ear again. "—should you."

Before her lips made contact with Star's ear, Star turned her head and drank her drink quickly. Not the most discreet movement, but she hoped the others wouldn't think twice about it.

"What did you do there?" Lissa sounded genuinely interested. Star turned toward the bar.

"I taught English."

"That's nice."

*

Lissa hoped her smile was polite, without tension, and that she didn't come off as awkward as she felt. "Well, I should get back to work." She felt ridiculous. Of course Star had a girlfriend. Star was *normal. Unlike Lissa.*

She sighed and jumped off the barstool, ignoring Star and Malena. She took her drink with her and went closer to the stage. It didn't help, she couldn't focus on the people on the stage. The band was all men, except for one female singer. They sounded okay, it wasn't their fault that Lissa was dying to turn around and look at Star again. Every cell in her—

"Liking that drink?" It was Malena again. "It has such a lovely yellow color."

"It's a lemon drop." Lissa took another sip. "The only drink I truly enjoy. It's so sweet and tart." She was rambling, but Malena didn't seem to mind.

"Sweet like you." Malena winked but managed to come off as more joking than flirtatious.

"So how come you've never been to Portugal? With your Dad and all? If I had a Dad who was Portuguese, I would have demanded to move there." Malena laughed, showing off her pearly whites.

It was a personal question. At least to Lissa, but the look on Malena's face wasn't prying or nosy. She looked friendly and curious. It made Lissa want to answer.

"He didn't like Portugal, and we never had the money to go anyway." It was the truth. She decided to keep her dad's political rants to herself. He had never agreed with the coup that overturned the government in the 1970s. In fact, he had disagreed so much, he had moved countries.

"Maybe you could still go." Malena bumped their hips together. "People change. Or you could go without him."

"I'd have to." It was hard to keep sadness and regret out of her voice. "He died a few years ago."

*

Star couldn't take her eyes off the way Lissa and Malena seemed to lock eyes as they kept talking. She could only see how beautiful Lissa was in the dim light of the bar; she had dimples for crying out loud. Illegally adorable.

Malena had noticed.

She was just Malena's type too. Despite Malena and Star's occasional flings, Malena usually went for the young and the cute. Skinny. Long hair. Feminine. Girly.

Lissa wasn't Star's type. *She is really, really not your type, so what is up with you?*

Malena wasn't unpleasant. She wasn't pushy. She was nice, sweet, and Star had never seen anything that hinted that Malena was anything but decent to the women she dated and slept with. Very open and honest. But the hand that ran up and down Lissa's arm agitated Star like nothing else. The worst part was that Lissa didn't seem to mind. Star bit her lip, the fine hairs on her arms standing up.

What's wrong with you? Stop acting like an idiot. Her fists clenched when she watched Lissa laugh at something Malena had said. *Maybe I'm ill?* What had Star expected when she found her in the bar? That they would dance in the dark? Have an intimate conversation by the bar where they would have to lean really close to hear what…

"Who is that girl?" Malena was back. "Are the two of you close? I'm surprised you shook your head at me earlier."

"We're just friends, it would feel weird. She's not even my type." *So why do you want her smile directed at you, you big idiot? Why are you already dreaming of the way her kisses would feel?* "You know me, I like them tall and voluptuous and…" Her eyes again were drawn toward Lissa's lean shape. She was clearly female with a small, high chest and a shy roundness around her hips but she wasn't—

Lissa turned her head a bit when she saw that Star was looking. She smiled.

"Ugh, this place is dead." Malena said in her ear. "Want to go back to my place?" Her arms snaked their way around Star's waist.

Star shook her head. She wanted to stay there and watch Lissa, but she couldn't say that out loud.

"Sorry, not tonight." She sighed. "I have work in the morning, and it's easier to get there from my place." She was lying and she didn't know why. She squeezed Malena's hand and stepped out of her embrace. "Why don't you go and find somebody to dance with?"

Malena rolled her eyes at her, but went into the small crowd to find somebody else to spend the night with. Star went back to the bar, wanting to order another drink.

"I like this place."

Star lifted her head, her heart skipping a beat. Lissa was standing there with a crooked grin on her face. There was a spark in her eyes that hadn't been there before.

"Finished working?"

"Yeah." Lissa sat down next to her. "So I came to check up on you." An unfamiliar pounding started in Star's chest, as if her heart was beating in staccato rhythm.

"You didn't have to."

"Of course I didn't have to." Lissa bumped their shoulders together. "I wanted to."

Star smiled to herself and looked into her glass. Unfamiliar shyness filled her being. She didn't even look up, didn't stare Lissa down like she usually would. Instead she felt unsure at what she would say or do. She wanted to say something that would blow Lissa's mind. Make her laugh. Make her think that she was smart.

"Are you and Malena… together?" Lissa sounded somewhere between curious and accusing.

"No." Star said quickly. "Well…"

"You've slept together." Lissa's voice betrayed no emotion. Not even jealousy.

"Yeah." *More than once.* "We've been friends all our lives basically, sometimes more than friends."

"But, you're not… girlfriends?"

Star looked at her. There was a sadness in her eyes but otherwise she looked normal. Almost blank. Star wanted to know what she was thinking.

"No, I'm not her type."

"But she's yours?"

Star and Lissa both turned their heads to look at Malena, who was now on the dance floor. Star took in the swaying blonde hair, the generous hip and chest. The openly sexual energy, the wide smile. Yes. Malena was definitely her type. So why was it that with both of them in the room, she only had eyes for Lissa?

"Yes. I mean…" *What can I say?*

"She's not mine." Lissa swallowed the last in her glass. "I think I like slightly more tomboy-ish women. I think."

"You think?" Star raised one of her eyebrows. "You don't *know*?"

Lissa placed her glass on the counter.

"I've never said I'm the most experienced girl around, you know?"

Star laughed at that.

Most of her friends were dancing now, and the music had gotten slightly louder. Suddenly, she felt bothered by it all. The music, the dim lights, the fact that it was getting harder and harder to hear what Lissa was saying. And Star wanted to hear what Lissa had to say.

"Hey, wanna get out of here?"

Lissa's mouth dropped open but quickly broke into a smile.

"I live about 10 minutes from here," she leaned forward so Star could hear what she was saying. "We could watch a movie or something."

Star nodded, trying to ignore the bells that rang in her head and chest. Finished her drink in one go and put her glass on the counter.

"Let me just say bye to Malena."

CHAPTER SIX

"I'll call you tomorrow, okay?" Star reached out, grabbed Malena's hand, and squeezed it.

Malena nodded, the way she was staring at Star made Lissa's heart pound. It was a mix of friendship and intimacy, and Lissa didn't think that anyone would ever look at her that way.

"Nice to meet you again." She held out her hand to shake Malena's, but Malena ignored it and instead pulled her into a quick hug.

"It was my pleasure. Any friend of Star's is a friend of mine." Malena looked sort of surprised to see them leaving together, but if she was, she didn't mention it.

They stepped outside.

"Are you sure it's fine that you left?" Lissa had to ask. "You and Malena seem really close. And we don't—"

Star stopped looking at her and shook her head with a small chuckle.

"You're right," she said. "We have just met and you don't really know me. If you did, you would have known that I very often leave parties like this, suddenly. Most of the times to go home with some girl."

"I'm not—" Lissa started to say, but Star cut her off.

"I know you're not." Her voice was gentle. "But Malena doesn't know that. And I wanted to leave." She chuckled again. "So don't worry about what anybody thought, okay?"

"Okay." Lissa was eager to let it go. She was happy that Star had suggested they leave. She wanted Star all to herself.

Since Lissa only lived a few blocks away, they decided to just walk rather than look for a bus or a taxi. They walked in silence, Lissa changing focus from the people back in the party to worried that she had left dirty laundry on the bedroom floor or what Star would even think about her studio apartment. Or the poster over her bed with the Disney princesses engaging in indecent acts.

It had been raining before, but it had mostly dried now and the sky was clear, a thousand stars looking down at them. Lissa started to feel light, as if she could skip down the road instead of just walking. She felt very aware of everything. Of the cool, damp air against her face and hands, of the sound and feel of her feet on the concrete. She knew that she had drank and that part of her giddiness was because of the alcohol, but she still relished the feeling of being very alive. For once, she didn't think about work.

"What movie do you want to watch?" Star kept looking ahead, her facial expression not visible in the dark.

"I don't know, something fun." Lissa smiled into the night. "I want to laugh."

"Laughing is good."

They arrived at Lissa's place and took the six flights of stairs up to her apartment. They would have taken the elevator but it wasn't downstairs.

"Maybe the door has jammed," Lissa said thoughtfully as they climbed the first flight of stairs. "It happens sometimes. It's an old elevator."

"It's good that I'm in such a great shape then." Star grinned.

Lissa laughed and rolled her eyes. It wasn't like she hadn't noticed. *I wonder if it's because she likes working out or because of her job.*

"I hope my place isn't super messy," she said, to think about something else.

Star laughed.

"Don't worry so much."

They finally reached Lissa's floor. She fumbled with the keys but finally got them into the lock. They went inside.

"This is where I live." She stood to the side, holding the door open for Star to enter.

"Nice." Star pushed her hands into her pockets as she regarded Lissa's home. "The poster." She let out a surprised laugh as she pointed towards the poster over the bed.

"Yeah." Lissa laughed too but felt her cheeks heat up. "It was a gift." It sounded lame to her own ears, even if it was the truth.

She looked at Star. Star was standing in her apartment, hands still in the pockets of her cargo pants, smiling and laughing at her poster. *This is beyond unreal.*

"Do you want a drink? I mean, I only have juice."

"Some juice would be great, yeah."

Lissa nodded as she headed towards the fridge, happy to have something to occupy her for a few moments.

"Do you want orange, carrot, or raspberry?"

"You weren't kidding around when you said you have juice." She could hear Star picking on her things behind her. "Raspberry?"

"Good choice." She returned to Star with the juice.

Star was standing in front of her bookcase, looking at Lissa's arbitrary collection of books, movies, and trinkets. She touched the rainbow colored slinky quickly. Lissa wanted to know what she was thinking but said nothing. Instead she sat down on the sofa, across from the bookcase, sipped on her juice, and enjoyed the view.

"Umm… Lissa?" Star straightened her back and turned around. "What is this?"

"Oh, that!" Lissa swallowed what she had in her mouth. "That's just a board game."

"*The Crazy Cow Game*?" Star raised one of her eyebrows.

"Yes." Lissa nodded. "It's hilarious. Wanna play?" The words were out of her mouth before she could stop them. "You're supposed to move cows to pasture, first to move five cows wins."

"You're so weird, I love it." Star sat down next to Lissa. "Sure, let's play."

Lissa opened the box and set it up while she explained.

"Okay, you have to go from the farmhouse to the field. Take a random cow card and move that card to pasture. We roll the dice and get different cards with missions we have to do to move our cows forward."

"I'll figure it out as we go along." Star nodded, seemingly eager to start.

"Which game piece do you want?" She held out the options and Star took one without looking.

They placed them on the farmhouse.

"You start, since it's your first time." Lissa felt giddy as she placed the dice in Star's hand. "Try to get a six; if you get a six, you can pick your cow card right away."

"I've done a lot of strange things in my time," Star rolled the dice, "but I think this takes the cake. Oh damn, four."

"Don't worry, you'll get there." Lissa grabbed the dice and flicked it across the table. She hadn't played the game for years, but it was still so much fun. "Yes! Six!"

Star mocked a sigh. "The house always wins. I should have known."

"Don't be silly. You'll get your first cow card this time, I'm sure."

Star laughed. A wide, happy sound that was different from the others that had escaped her mouth earlier. The sound was so joyous it made Lissa warm up inside.

"I never thought I'd say this, but I really hope I get my cow soon."

Lissa giggled.

"Okay, roll the dice."

On the next round, Star indeed got her cow card and the game could start for real. Lissa enjoyed how Star kept a wide smile on her face as they played. By chance, Star got ahead, and she was the first one to land on an action card.

"What should I do now?"

"Grab one of those and read what it says." Lissa pointed at the stack of cards that she had placed in the middle of the board. She mentally crossed her fingers while Star grabbed the one on top. She hoped that it wouldn't be something terribly cringe-inducing.

"*Your cow has been stung by a bee*," Star read out loud. "*You need to dance your own special bee-repelling dance. Let the other players judge if you pass or fail.* Oh, my."

"Still happy we're playing?" Lissa chuckled nervously, hoping that Star wasn't regretting agreeing to play the game too much.

"Hey, I'm an actress." Star winked. "I think a special bee-repelling dance is within my abilities."

She stood up, sighed dramatically, and then started jumping around the table, waving her arms around. Her facial expression was completely serious, which made the whole scene even more amusing. Lissa tried to not laugh, but pretty soon tears worked their way down her cheeks just from the effort.

Star sat down in front of her again.

"Did I pass?"

Lissa could only nod, she was laughing so much. Instead of answering, she threw the dice. She passed Star and landed on another action card.

"Can I see what it says?" Star pulled the card from Lissa's hands, the look on her face very eager. "Oh, that's boring."

"Go back three spaces. Well, it can't always lead to funny dances, can it?" Lissa moved her cow back three spaces.

"How come you have this game anyway?" Star threw the dice and moved her cow. She took a sip from her glass and handed the dice to Lissa.

"I've had it since I was a child. We used to play it: Mom, Dad, my sister, and I." The memory made Lissa smile. It felt normal. A completely natural development that she had once played this game with her parents and now played with Star. Like it was something that was always going to happen. It was the first time she had unpacked the game since their passing, and she wasn't even sad. She was just filled with giddy happiness.

"But you kept it."

Lissa touched the frail edge of the board, worn with time.

"We used to play it a lot. When they died and I got rid of their things, I couldn't get rid of it. This is the first time I've actually played it though."

Star's mouth fell open, and she looked down as if seeing the board for the first time.

"Thank you for playing it with me."

"No, thank *you*." Lissa handed the dice to Star. "Now, roll the dice."

Star rolled them while looking at Lissa. Their gazes met. Star's smile was open, friendly, not teasing and crooked like usual.

Star's phone rang. While she answered, Lissa got up from the sofa. *Gosh, what is up with me? What is up with us?* She grabbed their almost empty glasses and took them to the kitchenette to fill them again. She needed to cool down. She also wanted to give Star some privacy as well, and not listen to her phone call.

"No, not tomorrow. Next week. Yeah, okay. Fine. Bye."

Lissa didn't mean to listen in, but in the small space it was impossible not to hear what Star was saying.

"They wanted me to work tomorrow." Star pocketed her phone.

"Oh." Lissa sat down, unsure what to say. As the night had gone on, she had gotten more and more uncomfortable when thinking about Star's job. She couldn't reconcile the anonymous person she had watched on her computer screen and the living, breathing woman in front of her.

"But I'm not working tomorrow, they had the wrong date."

"Do you like your job?" The question popped out of her mouth before she could stop it.

Star grinned.

"Yeah, I've loved almost every minute of it."

"Almost?" Lissa turned her head to the side. "What didn't you like?"

Star sucked in air through her nose. "Once I did a movie with a man, we only shared a kiss and a woman, but that one I didn't in particular like."

"Yeah, I can imagine that." Lissa grabbed her glass and drank, trying to act casual.

"And, I mean." Star seemed to think. "I do it because I enjoy it, but there are some who only do it for the money. Like straight girls who are clearly not into what I'm doing to them. That always sucks."

"What do you do then?" Lissa leaned forward. She had a hard time imagining anyone not enjoying their time with Star.

"My job of course. What I am paid to do." Star's voice momentarily got an edge to it. "We performed, but it wasn't nice to know that she was mainly faking her pleasure."

"It must have been hard." Lissa had drank so much of her juice now in attempt to act normal that her bladder was letting itself be known. "Umm… I'll be right back. Excuse me."

*

Lissa hurried away from the table and walked through a door that Star assumed led to the bathroom. *Did I make her uncomfortable?* It was hard to know with Lissa. One minute she was asking questions, trying so hard not to seem interested—her blush and wide eyes made that clear—but the next she clammed up, and seemed to want to run away.

She didn't mind indulging Lissa's curiosity. But not if it made Lissa uncomfortable with her.

A toilet flushed, the tap ran, and then the door opened again.

"Sorry," Lissa smiled coyly. "I'm back."

"No problem. Should we keep playing?" Star gestured toward the board.

Lissa nodded.

"Roll the dice."

They played for a bit longer, neither of them saying anything. Star was surprised how relaxed she felt. She wasn't a shy person, usually comfortable in big crowds or small crowds. It wasn't until she was here with Lissa that she realized that she was always in character. She always carried her cocksure, on-camera persona with her. She had surrounded herself with people who were involved in the same type of business or who were involved with someone who was involved in the same business. She hadn't known how it felt to be completely relaxed until she was.

Star checked the dice and moved her cow four spaces. She handed the dice to Lissa but didn't allow her fingers to linger.

Lissa kept sipping her drink as they played, and when she picked her next action card, she still had liquid in her mouth. Her eyes grew wide and she coughed as she tried to not splutter.

"What?" Star reached out, trying to take the card from her.

"Nothing, nothing, let me just change the…" Lissa tried to keep the card from Star and aimed to put it on the bottom of the pile, but Star snagged it from her grip.

She took one look at it and burst out laughing.

"*There is a kissing noodle on the road,*" she read out loud. "What the 'eff is a kissing noodle? *Quickly kiss the person on your right before your cow runs ten steps back.*"

Lissa's face was completely red and her bottom lip was quivering. Star's annoyance with her question quickly ran away to be exchanged by something clutching on her heart.

"You can kiss me." She didn't know what made her say the words. *Please, kiss me.* She wanted to know what it was like. To be kissed by someone like Lissa. Someone so sweet, so… Lissa.

"I want to." The words were whispered. Lissa's eyes bored into Star's.

The rest of the world faded away until all Star was aware of was the beating of her heart and the deer-in-headlight look in Lissa's face. Lissa was looking increasingly terrified and Star was starting to pity her.

"You don't have to, Lissa, I was joking. Just put the—"

Star fell silent when Lissa leapt from her seat on the floor and sat down next to her on the sofa. They both stayed silent as Lissa framed Star's face with both hands and then proceeded to give her the sweetest and most careful kiss that Star had ever received.

The game was probably meant for children, and the card probably called for a peck on the cheek, but Lissa had zoned in on her lips. It was just a fleeting touch, but it had Star panting and sweating and unsure of what to do with herself.

When Lissa pulled back, she had a coy smile of triumph on her face as she moved back to her own seat. Picked up her drink and sipped it. It was only the ever-present blush and her avoidant gaze that showed Lissa had been affected by the kiss too.

"Did I pass?"

"Huh?" Star had no idea what Lissa meant.

"Do I need to move my cow back ten spaces?" Lissa looked up, her eyes glittering, her smile teasing. "Or did my kiss pass the test?"

"Oh, you passed." Star was rather enjoying the feeling of being out of her depth and being teased, but she couldn't help to crook her smile and lean forward until Lissa's cocksure smile disappeared.

That'll teach her to mess with me. Star wanted to laugh again.

"I want to watch more." Lissa's words almost made Star drop the dice.

"Wha... what?" There was no way that Lissa was saying what Star thought she was saying.

"I want to watch something else that you have done. Could you point me in the right direction?"

It took a while until Star could get her vocal cords to work.

"Yes. Yes, I can do that. I'll leave you some links, or we could find a..." Star wanted to bite her lip before the words came out of her mouth, "we could find a fan site that has lots of clips or GIFs. If you prefer. I know of at least one."

"*Fan site?*"

"Yeah." Star cringed internally, unsure what Lissa would think about the fact that somebody had made a fan site of her fucking.

"Okay." Lissa just nodded, her facial expression betraying nothing. "Let's find a fan site." She looked at Star with a pointed look in her face.

"What? Right now?"

Lissa grabbed her glass and chugged the rest of the contents. Her nervous behavior with the glass was starting to get on Star's nerves. She just wanted to grab it from her and tell her to stop beating around the bush and just say what it was that she wanted to say.

"Yeah." Her face was still completely red. It almost impressed Star that she was still saying these things, expressing her interest when her discomfort and embarrassment were almost tangible.

This girl is something else. Oh, the things Star could teach her. Show her. She wanted to make that mouth tremble with anticipation. Give her other things to blush about. Make her tremble and want and...

Star mentally chastised herself. This was her new, young friend. It wasn't a hook-up. Lissa almost seemed to *like* her at times and that was dangerous. Star wasn't looking for a relationship. "Do you have a computer?" *Let's do this.* Just because they weren't going to date didn't mean that Star couldn't have some fun with her. *Safe fun.*

Lissa grabbed her laptop from under the sofa, put in her password in, and then handed it to Star.

It took a moment for Star to react after the unabashed behavior. Laughter was bubbling in her chest. Maybe it was the earlier alcohol, or the whole strange game night, or maybe simply the fact that she was getting silly-tired.

Their eyes met over the rim of Lissa's laptop and they both chuckled in the same time.

"This is so weird." Star opened a web browser and searched for her screen name with the words "fan site" after. She knew they existed. Most of the time she was proud of it. "Just remember that I'm not doing this because I'm nice. I'm doing this because I feel responsible to provide you with good adult entertainment. Can't have you searching for it yourself and seeing something bad quality. Or worse, straight porn."

She clicked on the familiar link and handed it back to Lissa. Then she stood up.

"You check it out, I need to use the bathroom. Was it this door?"

Lissa nodded mindlessly, her eyes on the screen. Star grinned and headed to the bathroom.

*

Lissa was grateful that Star had gone to the bathroom, giving her some time to look at the site by herself.

I don't know what I'm doing. Am I flirting with her? Am I simply curious? Lissa didn't know. She usually moved in a world where outwards confidence was everything, whether you had it or not. She was so used to smiling and talking until she got her way, until she convinced people that she knew she could do what she did. She didn't know what was wrong with her around Star.

She looked at the screen, her heart hammering in her chest. The first posts were just photos of Star in different poses. Usually when you saw people in magazines or in modeling situations, it was somebody unreal. Somebody *out there.* Not somebody in your bathroom.

One photo-shoot especially, of Star topless, in cargo pants, lying lazily on a chair, staring into the camera, made Lissa's chest grow hot. She curled her hand under the rim of the sofa, needing to hold on to something.

She scrolled down and got to the first GIF. Star was lying on her back, a woman between her legs and Star's hand on her head.

The toilet flushed in the bathroom, and Lissa hurriedly continued scrolling, wanting to see as much as possible before Star came back. She needed to be ready when Star returned, she needed feign some disinterest. She couldn't let Star know how interested she was.

As she kept scrolling, a few things became completely clear in Lissa's mind. Star had done stuff that Lissa could never even imagine herself doing. Things that she wasn't interested in even trying. Things that involved pain or leather.

It was also clear that Star had slept with a hell of a lot of people. Just in the first few pages, Star had been filmed or photographed with over ten different people, and in some photos, she was with more than two women at once. So far away from Lissa's own world.

In one way Lissa wished she hadn't asked to see more. She wanted to see more, but she also wanted to keep seeing Star as a human. As a normal woman who—

The toilet flushed, and Lissa slapped her laptop closed almost as a reflex. Which was completely stupid since Star knew what site she had been on.

"You liked what you saw?" Star sat down in front of her. The look in her face made Lissa want to punch her. It was something more than smugness.

"Yes." No use in beating around the bush, but at least her tone wasn't shaking. "Well, mostly."

"Mostly," Star repeated. "Fair enough." She laughed but then looked sober. "I'm planning to quit quite soon though."

"Why? Because of the age thing?"

Star chuckled. "I'm bored, can you believe it? I've saved up loads of money too, I think it's just time for me to move on. I'm just wrapping up a few old projects and that's that."

"Okay." Lissa nodded. "What are you gonna do after?"

"No idea." Star pulled a hand through her short buzz. "Study, maybe. I have no idea what I want to do, despite having copious amounts of sex."

Lissa coughed.

"I'm joking. Well, mostly." Star grinned. "It's so good though, you know?"

Is she actually asking me?

"Well, I…" Lissa bit her lip.

"What?"

Lissa shook her head. She wouldn't tell. Not Star. Not anyone really, but definitely not Star.

"Star?" She asked before Star had a chance to ask about her withheld facts.

"Yes?"

"Are we friends?"

Star's eyes went wide and a small smile graced her lips.

"Yeah, I think we're becoming friends. Why?"

Lissa's somehow felt both shy and determined.

"It makes me happy to consider you my friend. But also…" She pulled air into her nose, slowly. "I want to meet you again. I want to do exactly this. Laugh. Play silly games. Have fun."

The look of surprised joy on Star's face was everything. Lissa smiled as well. She was going to say something else but was suddenly overcome by a yawn.

"Aww, tired I guess?" Star took up her glass and downed the contents. The action was final, as if she was planning to get up and go.

"Yeah. It's pretty late." Lissa didn't want her to go.

Star glanced on her phone.

"Wow, yeah, it's three in the morning." She put it back in her pocket. "I should go."

"You can sleep on the sofa." Lissa's heart pounded away and she hoped that Star didn't think she was coming on to her. "It's late after all." *And I don't want you to go yet.*

Star looked like she was thinking for a while.

"Okay." She nodded. "Thank you, that would be great."

"Great." Lissa stood up. Then she looked down at the table. "Oh, our game." Apparently, they had both forgotten.

"We'll keep playing sometime." Star searched for her gaze. "I promise."

*

Lissa seems to have gone out like a light, Star thought as she lay on the sofa under the blanket. The fridge kept making a buzzing noise that made it hard to sleep and she had too many thoughts occupying her mind.

It was nice to not have to go home. Lissa's place was so much more intimate than Star's fancy place, and the sound of Lissa's breathing soothed her.

She turned on her side and looked at the figure in the bed at the alcove. She couldn't see her from her position, but she knew she was there. She could also hear her soft breathing. Star smiled to herself. Lissa was fun. And cute. It was impossible to think they hadn't known each other just a few days ago.

I should take her on a date. The thought came out of the blue and Star groaned. She couldn't just ask Lissa out, could she? What would they even do?

Go dancing. Star's pained grimace was replaced with a smile in the dark. She imagined dancing with Lissa in the dark space of a club, the thumping beat filling their bodies. Moving closer. Kissing.

"Oh." Star was surprised over the level of arousal her little vision gave her. She wanted to take Lissa dancing, yes. Goad out smile after smile from Lissa's face, yes. But more than anything she wanted to kiss her again.

The small peck during the game hadn't been enough. Star wanted more. Too bad she couldn't have it.

*

They stood by the door, their recently emptied plates on the table by the sofa. Lissa couldn't believe that they had arrived here. At goodbye. They had been talking about resuming their run of *The Crazy Cow Game,* but Star's phone had rung and she had said that she needed to hurry.

Lissa didn't know what to say. And the look in Star's face suggested that she was equally speechless. She bit her lip and Lissa almost worried—hoped—that Star would try to kiss her. Which was ridiculous, they were just friends.

"We'll see each other soon, yes?"

Lissa nodded. *I hope so.*

"This is ridiculous." Star shook her head and grinned at Lissa. "Why is it so hard to leave?"

Lissa giggled.

"Maybe…" Her breath caught as Star leaned forward and pressed a longer than necessary kiss to her cheek.

"Bye." Star turned around and left through the door, not closing it after herself.

Lissa stood in the open door as if she was paralyzed, listening to the footsteps of Star in the stairs. It was only when it had been silent for a good five minutes that Lissa realized that they hadn't even exchanged numbers.

CHAPTER SEVEN

"I'm here." It was the next day, and Star walked through a corridor covered in photographs of a smiling woman with long blonde hair; someone very different from the grey creature inside the living room, even though they were the same person. Hawke Ciel, Star's mother, didn't even look up when Star entered the room.

Hawke's nurse was sitting next to her with a soup bowl on her lap.

"Helen, you need to eat something."

"She prefers the name Hawke, you know that." Star tried to have patience with her Mom's nurses, but sometimes it was hard.

"It doesn't matter what I call her, she won't eat." The newest nurse, Natasha, sounded as though she had completely given up. "Nobody has gotten her to eat in over 24 hours. I think we need to go back to the hospital. She'll waste away if this continues."

"She hates the hospital." Star knelt in front of her mom. Looked into the green eyes that had once looked back at her with recognition. "Mom? You need to eat something." She sighed. "Hawke, this is important. If you don't eat, I'll have to take you to the hospital, and you don't want that. I know you don't."

She took the bowl from Natasha, scooped up some soup on the spoon, and blew on it.

"This smells delicious, Hawke. You'll like it, I promise." *Come on, Mom.*

Hawke looked like she was going to start crying, but, keeping her eyes on Star, she opened her mouth and let Star feed her.

"Good, Hawke. Perfect."

She managed to feed her Mom seven spoonfuls of soup before Hawke blatantly refused to open her mouth again.

"She needs more," Natasha hissed.

"I know." Star ran her hand over Hawke's grey-blonde hair. "And we'll try again in 30 minutes. But she's done well for now. Would you turn on the TV for her?"

Natasha just sighed and walked over to the TV to grab the remote. It didn't matter what program it was. Hawke didn't have enough presence to notice. But she fixed her eyes on it, and Star preferred that to her mom staring into nothing.

"Thanks for calling me, Natasha." Star stood up. "I'll stay for 30 minutes and we'll try to feed her again. Then I need to go home and take a shower. When is your shift ending?"

"My shift ends at four." It was several hours until then. "Lindsey starts her shift at four-twenty."

"Good." Star nodded. "I'll come back at three and we'll try to get her to eat again before you leave."

"Very good, miss." Natasha sounded tired. Star understood that feeling.

Star stretched her back and looked around the room. She really needed to hire some kind of housekeeper. *Or clean it myself, I suppose.* Natasha and the other nurses didn't let it get that bad; they occasionally swept the floors and took out the trash, but that was it. Hawke's living room was barren. No flowers, no books, just a stack of dusty magazines next to her armchair. They were still there even though Hawke hadn't had the energy to read one for over a year. Star promised herself that she would read one for her next time she was over.

"I appreciate you, Natasha," Star said in a low voice. "I can tell you always do your best, even when she's being difficult."

"Thank you." Natasha smiled. "I'll clean up in the kitchen."

Star got a stool and sat down next to her mom, took her hand. Squeezed it.

"I'm here, Mom. For a little while."

CHAPTER EIGHT

It was Tuesday.

Tuesday.

Lissa yawned. She hated Tuesdays. It wasn't the bearable start of Mondays where you received new projects or planned out the week, it wasn't the stress of Wednesday or Thursday when you were trying to get everything together for the big day that was on Friday or Saturday. Though Lissa wasn't too happy about her job on any day anymore, Tuesdays were days of tedious phone calls or paperwork.

And dreaming about Star.

Lissa leaned back on her chair and chewed on the back of her pencil. Yes, thinking about Star was definitely a nice addition to her boring day. The client, Mrs. Ramsey, wanted Lissa to plan a birthday party for her twin daughters. Children's parties were the dreariest to plan, it was a balance to make both parents and kid happy.

"I wonder what Star would pick," Lissa said out loud to herself, "chocolate or vanilla." She sat up and wrote *cake* on her notebook. "Maybe she would pick a tiger cake with both. Swirls."

You're pathetic, Lissa. You need to stop thinking about a woman so out of your league.

She grabbed her phone, planning to call the bakery to order a tiger cake with chocolate frosting in the shape of a... *Star*. She smiled to herself. Pathetic or not, she deserved little moments of silliness. The client didn't need to know why the cake was in the shape of a star, she would probably just like it.

The phone in her hand buzzed and she looked down, expecting it to be the client back with even more demands. She read the first words on the notification, feeling puzzled. It was an unknown number. She clicked on it, her heart pounding as she read.

Hey, Lissa. I got your number from the business card you gave me, I hope you don't mind. I was thinking about our poor cows that still haven't made their way to pasture. Maybe we should keep playing soon. Or maybe I should buy you dinner first. Not out of the goodness of my heart, of course, but because I worry you'll eat the cow otherwise and I can't live with that on my conscience.

Lissa laughed out loud, the dreariness of Tuesday immediately floating away. She couldn't believe that Star had tracked down her number. Well, she could believe it, but it was still a pleasant surprise. She hurried to answer. It took less than a minute for her phone to *pling* with another message from Star.

Sounds good. Friday?

Wow, she's eager. Lissa grinned. She was about to answer when she glanced at the papers she had on the desk. *Fuck.* She couldn't. Not with a party on Saturday.

Sorry. I have work this weekend. But on the following weekend?

It sucked, but at least she would have something to look forward to while planning a party for a couple of five-year-olds who wouldn't be able to appreciate it fully. She waited patiently for Star's answer.

Blech. Stupid work, right? But sure, I'm free. It's a date. Friday next week.

Lissa didn't know what she could answer that didn't express the illogical level of happiness she was feeling. Her cheeks stained, as she couldn't stop smiling, and her heart fluttered in her chest. She stared at the word *date*. She knew what that word meant. But she couldn't remember being this nervous north of fifteen.

She put her phone away, ready to get back to business. She looked at her notebook, saw the word *cake* scribbled there. She took out her work phone and called the bakery.

CHAPTER NINE

"Listen to me." Chause gesticulated wildly. "What I want for this scene is fear, but not creepy fear. More like a nervousness that is chased away by being so aroused that…"

Star's phone, stuffed into her discarded jeans, started vibrating in the corner. Chause, the director, fell silent and looked at Star and her co-worker with a questioning look on her face.

"Sorry," Star said, "I forgot to turn it off, I'll do it before we start filming. Go ahead." She ran the tips of her fingers along Alanya's spine, trying to get them to be comfortable with each other. She had met Alanya before, but they had never done anything together. Star couldn't help but look forward to it, Alanya looked *delicious.*

"As I was saying," Chause continued but stopped almost right away as Star's phone started vibrating once more.

"This isn't a vibrator scene," Alanya whispered with a silly smile.

"Shut up." Star shook her head. "Excuse me." She got up from her position on the bed, walked over to her jeans, and found her phone.

She had two missed calls from Laurel, another one of Hawke's nurses. Before she had had the time to turn around and excuse herself, *clearly she had to call Laurel back,* her phone vibrated in her hand. But it was Natasha this time, not Laurel. *What the hell?*

Her heart began to beat in a scared staccato rhythm as Star answered without even excusing herself.

"Natasha, what's wrong? Laurel called me—"

"Star, you need to come here. Hawke has…" Natasha sobbed. "One of her old friends came over with a bottle of whisky. We think she swallowed pills too. She isn't breathing."

The world stood still. Even Star's raging heart seemed to quiet. Star took one slow breath, closed her eyes.

"She's dead." It was a statement, not a question. There was something comfortable in accepting the truth, a truth she had been—

"Not yet."

"What?"

"We're rushing her to Heart Center Hospital, can you come?"

"Of course." Star didn't say anything more. She knew where Heart Center Hospital was. She knew where she was needed.

"What's happened?" Chause was looking at her. Alanya said nothing, but looked worried.

"I've got to go." Star couldn't even look at them, she just managed an "I'm sorry, I'll explain later," before she had pulled her jeans on.

"You can't just leave!" Chause got up from his chair and walked towards her. "We have everything set up, you—"

"My mom is in the hospital," Star said through gritted teeth. "Bill me, fire me, I don't care. I need to go."

She was barely present as she got out of the room, out of the building. She hailed a cab with her hand. She hadn't known it was possible to feel like this. Like her mind was racing and empty in the same time.

That's not true, you know this feeling. The mind-numbing pain and shock. The helplessness and anger. They were feelings she had gotten last time Hawke had tried to kill herself. And the time before that. And the time before that.

"Where to, miss?"

A cab had stopped and she had gotten into it, all on autopilot. She couldn't stop her thoughts from spinning out of control. She honestly didn't know if she wanted Hawke to die or not.

*

Star paid the driver and ran toward the entrance of the hospital. The 'Information Desk' sign seemed to dance in front of her, like a mirage. How she was still walking she didn't know; she was a sweaty, pounding mess.

"Hawke... Helen Ciel, my mother. She's been brought in for..." Star swallowed past the lump in her throat. "Um, she drank too much. Pills." *What department did you go to for a botched suicide attempt?*

"Let me check." The nurse typed something on her computer. She had a kind smile, but when she asked for Star's ID, Star almost growled. "I'm sorry, it's standard procedure."

"What if I didn't have it on me?" Angry tears forced themselves down the corner of her eyes. She wanted to argue, be difficult, even though it was in her wallet like usual.

The nurse didn't answer.

Star got her ID out of her wallet and gave it to her. She barely registered her phone beeping for the umpteenth time. Her agent this time. Star turned it off. She didn't care about her career right now. *Let them hate me.*

"Thank you, Ms. Ciel. Your mother is still in the Intensive Care Unit." The nurse pointed to the right. "Follow this corridor, turn left, then follow the signs."

Star didn't answer, she just nodded. In some part of her brain, she registered that the nurse called the ICU and told them Helen Ciel's daughter was coming. She started half-running down the corridor, worried that she wouldn't manage to find her way. But at least they were expecting her.

Following the signs was thankfully not hard, even in her distressed state, and soon Star found herself by a locked door. She rang the bell and was let in as soon as she said who she was. Before she entered, they referred her to a small station where she washed her hands. After that, she was let into the ICU.

"Your mother is still with the doctor." She shook hands with a nurse.

"Can I see her?" They walked together down the corridor.

"No, she's unconscious right now and the doctor is busy." Star was shown into a small alcove with a couple of comfortable chairs. "Sit down here and we'll let you know as soon as something changes."

The nurse hurried away.

Star looked at the chairs in front of her. Her heart was still pounding and adrenaline was coursing through her veins. The idea of *sitting down* and just *waiting* was inconceivable. She was ready for fight or flight, not rest.

She walked over to the watercooler, grabbed a plastic cup, and filled it to the brim. She downed it in one go. Filled another one and did the same. It soothed her dry throat and made her body feel less heated. It didn't make her feel better, but she didn't think anything would. At least she was the only one waiting; she didn't think she could deal with other people right now.

She paced back and forth, glancing at the clock. It was already an hour since the original phone call from Natasha. *I have to call Chause and tell him...*

Star sighed and sank down on one of the chairs. The suspense was killing her. Maybe it would have been better if Star had just ignored the phone call and stayed there. What good could she do here anyway? There was no point. There was no way Hawke would survive this time. Her heart was probably too worn out.

She looked at the clock again. It had been less than five minutes. Star wanted to cry. She wanted to cry like a little child.

She fell forward, her head in her hands. *Mommy.* She didn't want her mom to die. She closed her eyes, sat up, and hit the back of her head to the wall. The time needed to go faster.

"Ms. Ciel?"

Star blinked a couple of times.

"Ms. Ciel?"

Her eyes focused on the man in front of her. He was wearing a white coat. *Doctor!* Star straightened her back and was right away focused.

"Yes," she said. "You have news about my mother?"

"The acute crisis is over, but she's still very weak. We have to keep monitoring her heart rate and breathing, but she's alive."

The world stopped.

"What?" Star wasn't sure she had heard correctly. "She's alive? But…"

"Her heart stopped several times," the doctor said matter-of-factly. "We brought her back, every time."

Star burst into tears.

"Couldn't you just have let her die?" Star knew she was acting crazy but couldn't help it. She felt like punching the doctor in the face. "She wanted to die, why… why…"

"Star!" Strong arms enveloped her from behind. It was Natasha. "Star, calm down."

Star pushed her arms away and got free.

"I'm sorry," she said through gritted teeth.

"Don't worry," the doctor said. "Like I said, she's stable now. You can go and see her."

Star was breathing hard, her hands trembling. It was almost nice to have Natasha next to her, like a caring big sister.

"Come on," Natasha's voice was warm, like honey. "You know you want to see her."

No, I don't.

"Laurel called me," Natasha said as she led Star to follow the doctor. "I came as soon as I could. Didn't think that Laurel wanted to stay. And I didn't want you to be here by yourself."

Every step was difficult, as if her legs were very tired.

"Stop dragging your feet," Natasha whispered to her. "You're acting like a child."

"My mom tried to kill herself," Star hissed back. "Again. I have the right to act like a child."

They finally got to Hawke's room.

"She might have difficulty talking," the doctor said as they entered.

"She always has difficulty talking." Star approached the sad figure on the bed.

Hawke's eyes were closed and the skin underneath was blue. Her lips were purple and on the top of her chest, just above the hospital gown, her skin looked paper-thin. She was connected to an EKG. Its beeps were the only thing showing that she was still alive. She looked more like a corpse than a woman.

Star took a hold of her hand, feeling guilty. Blaming herself.

"I'm sorry, Mom." Her hand was cold and sweaty, but it didn't matter because Star's was too.

Hawke's eyes opened and focused on Star's face.

"I'm sorry you didn't manage." Tears dripped off the tip of Star's nose and landed on Hawke's hand. "I'm sorry they saved you." Star didn't care if Natasha or the doctor heard her. "Better luck ne—"

"Star!" Natasha's warning echoed against the wall of the room.

"What?" Star yelled back. "She wants to die. We can't even grant her only wish? Are we that selfish?"

"I think you should leave the room," the doctor said in a stern voice. "Your mother needs rest. And you need to calm down."

"Fuck you all." Star fled the room.

*

"Malena?" Star couldn't keep the whining out of her voice. "Can you come here?" Malena hadn't actually answered her phone, but Star knew her friend would check her voicemail. She sobbed. "I don't know what to do with myself." She chugged another long sip from her vodka bottle. "Just come here. The door is unlocked." She turned off the call and threw her phone on the carpet.

CHAPTER TEN

Of all the parties I've ever planned—Lissa yawned—*this is by far the most boring.* Lissa enjoyed the thrill of a good party; the dressing up, the pretty people, cool food, and beating music. Hot dogs and Jonas Brother's hits weren't something she had signed up for. If the money hadn't been good.... At least she had enjoyed the cake. Lovely lemon and vanilla cream in the shape of a star. *Star.*

She locked her door and kicked off her shoes. At least the job was over and next weekend she wasn't working. The evening was over. She had done her duty. She dropped down on her bed before wrangling out of her pantyhose. She took up her laptop that was still lying there since this morning and balanced it on her thighs.

No emails, which was both a disappointment and relief. She wasn't ready to sleep yet, and the night stretched out before her. She missed Dea. If they had lived in the same town, she could have called her for an impromptu movie night.

Lissa sighed. Dea was probably with her boyfriend Grayson anyway. She had had increasingly little time for Lissa lately. Not that Lissa had had so much time for Dea anyway. She was too preoccupied with work. And confusing thoughts about Star.

Star. Just the thought of that elusive and interesting woman made her all warm inside. Lissa couldn't wait for next weekend when they were going to meet again.

She glanced at the button to access her computer's history. Hesitating, biting her lip. *You shouldn't.* It wasn't that she thought that Star would mind exactly, but it still felt wrong.

With her heart beating at the base of her throat, Lissa went to her computer history and clicked on the link to the fan site that Star had shown her a few days ago.

Fuck it. She turned around on her belly, pulled the computer closer, and pushed her hand into her panties. She might as well enjoy herself after such a day… and perhaps masturbating to porn that involved a friend was slightly immoral, but there were worse things to do. Like murdering someone. Or kicking a puppy.

She clicked on one of the videos and held her breath as it started. It was in the middle of a scene, two women were making out on a bed, Star sitting on a chair next to the bed reading a magazine and looking rather disinterested. Just the sight of her made Lissa wet and she teased herself, not really touching anything, just stoking the cautious emotions that were running through her.

The women on the bed were getting really eager, touching and moaning. The sounds did have an effect on her even though the sight of the women didn't. And Star's indifference was a turn-on too, even though Lissa couldn't exactly explain why. The way Star looked at the women, raised an eyebrow, and then continued reading sent thrills down Lissa's spine. She supposed it was a power thing. Star, in her indifference, held the power. Like the women were nothing. Lissa didn't even know why she found that fact so sexy. It was even sexier to think that just a week ago, those same eyes had looked at her with laughter and friendship in them.

"She's just acting, you goof," Lissa said to herself.

She had been so focused on Star that she hadn't even looked at the women. They had now lost their tops and one of them was fondling the other's breast. They weren't even that attractive. Not to Lissa. But maybe Star thought they were?

"Come on," one of the women said. "Trisha wants you so much, you need to take care of her better. Look at the state of her."

The woman underneath her, Trisha, looked almost desperate, her face flushed and her eyes barely open. Her naked chest rose and fell with each strained breath. Lissa wondered how much was just acting and how much was pure arousal.

"Shut up." Star got up, and instead of doing anything to Trish, she grabbed the other woman by the hair and pulled her closer. The woman whimpered and her eyes grew wide.

"You." Star's voice wasn't her own. It was darker, sharper. Lissa didn't like it. "You don't tell me what to do. Ever."

She lifted her hand as to slap her; the woman closed her eyes and—

Lissa closed of the lid of her laptop. She removed the hand from the base of her belly and felt sick. Why would Star do a video like that? Did she like it? Is that what sex was to Star? Is that what it had to be? She sobbed, suddenly close to tears. Her heart pounded.

It was Star on that video. Star with the funny comments and kind smile. Star who in spite of her scary and exciting career seemed so human. *Maybe I should cancel our date. If it even is a date. I'm way out of my depth with this one.*

She closed her eyes and tried to breathe deeply. She needed to calm down and think clearly.

Her phone beeped on top of her table.

Lissa looked at it, then she crawled out of her bed. She wiped her wet cheeks with the back of her hand as she went and got her phone. It was a text from Dea.

Got time to talk?
xoxo

Instead of answering by text, Lissa called her. Dea answered on the first ring.

"Hey." Dea sounded like her mouth was full of porridge, like she had been crying. All stuffy nose and sad voice. "Thanks for calling."

"You don't need to thank me for that." All thoughts of Star flew out of Lissa's head when she heard her sister's distress. "What's up?"

"Nothing really." Dea sighed loudly. "Just PMS, I think. I keep crying. And Grayson is being an idiot."

"What has he done now?" Lissa laid down on her bed again, propped up against the pillows, phone in hand. She ignored the wish to kick her laptop off of the bed. She didn't want to remember what site was on it.

"It's what he hasn't done." Dea sighed again. "It doesn't matter, I can't expect him to understand what I'm feeling, you know?"

"Not without telling him clearly," Lissa answered. "Don't assume he can read your mind. Grayson isn't used to thinking for himself." Whatever Dea saw in her idiotic friend, Lissa didn't know, but she still wanted to help.

"You don't get it." Dea wasn't really annoyed, she was being childish, and for once Lissa didn't have the energy to deal with it. She could see in her mind's eye Dea's pout and crossed arms. "Or have you gotten out of your voluntary celibacy and gotten yourself a girlfriend?"

Lissa sucked in air through her teeth.

"No girlfriend." Her heart beat so loud she worried that Dea would hear it. "There is… an interest." A giggle escaped. "It probably won't lead to anything but—"

"Why do you say it won't lead to anything?"

Lissa laughed for real now.

"You're not going to believe this," she said. All of a sudden she wanted to tell Dea about everything. "She's a porn star."

Silence.

"A… porn star?" Dea said. "You like a porn star? How did you meet?"

"At a party I planned." Lissa laid down on the bed with her phone in her hand. "We met there and talked a bit, then we ran into each other last week. I even played *The Crazy Cow Game* with her. I think we're becoming friends."

"Really?" Dea's voice gentled. "You must really like her if you played that with her."

"Yes." The word exited her mouth before she had fully thought about it. But it was the truth.

"So… are you girlfriends or…?"

"No!" Lissa felt her cheeks heat. "We're just friends. But I think we're becoming good friends." A wish to share entered her mind. "I like it. It's been a while since I made a new friend like this."

"But you like her, right? I mean, like her, like her." Dea's tone was still soft, as if she knew how difficult this was for Lissa. It made it easy for Lissa to admit everything.

"I do. But it scares me too."

"What scares you?"

Lissa inhaled slowly, remembering the video she had seen just a few minutes ago.

"That I'm out of my depth. That I'm a ridiculous child and she's an adult. That I won't be able to... umm... please her?" Now Lissa's face was on fire. "I saw one of her videos earlier, it was quite *advanced.*"

"Advanced?" Dea's tone of voice changed. "Well, it's her job, Liss. Have you asked about it?"

"No. I just saw it, no time to talk with her about it." Lissa chortled. "Like literally before you called me."

"Oh, Liss."

Lissa didn't like the sound of Dea's voice.

"What?"

"It's nice to hear that you like someone. Normal. You deserve it."

"I hear a 'but' coming."

Dea sighed.

"If her movies make you uncomfortable, I'm not sure she's good for you. What about sexually transmitted diseases?"

"Diseases?" Lissa repeated. "She mainly sleeps with women."

"Doesn't matter," Dea said. "Chlamydia and gonorrhea can be transmitted through toys too."

Lissa closed her eyes. Was Dea actually saying these words? Was it too much to ask to be met with happiness and understanding?

"Whatever." She pushed her own feelings down. "This was about Grayson, I'm sorry."

"Ugh, forget about him." There was a thud on the other end. Lissa could imagine Dea throwing her tennis ball against the wall. A classic symptom of Dea feeling annoyed or stressed. "I just need to stop waiting for him and ask him out myself."

"Exactly."

"And your relationship is what we should talk about!"

"It's not a relationship." Lissa hugged herself with the arm not holding her phone. "It's a new friendship."

"Whatever." Dea had turned back into her usual impatient self. "So when are you seeing her again?"

This time Lissa smiled in spite of the cautious tone in Dea's voice.

"We're going out next weekend."

"That's cool, I guess! Any idea of what you're going to do?" There was a noise in the background. "Oh, Sanna and Sara are here now. We're going to the cinema."

Lissa lifted her phone and glanced at the time.

"At midnight?"

"It's a late screening of *Dude, Where's My Car?*"

"Why… would you… never mind." Lissa shook her head and chuckled. "Have fun then."

"I will! Call me soon, okay? And seriously, be careful. I don't want you to get hurt."

"Okay."

They said their goodbyes and Lissa turned off the call. The terror had left her chest and she could breathe easier. Dea was right, after all. She didn't know what she had been thinking. Star was totally wrong for her. They would have to remain only friends.

She looked at her laptop again, lying by her feet. She was very tempted to pick it up and look for a more enjoyable video to watch before sleeping.

"Oh, hell with it." She hid her shame in the deepest part of her brain and grabbed the laptop again. She wanted to watch Star, so she would, come hell or high water.

CHAPTER ELEVEN

After agonizing over whether she should choose burgundy or forest green, Star grabbed the burgundy button-up shirt and paired it with her usual black slacks. She wasn't feeling like her usual self and felt that it was important to at least look her best. Even if her hair was growing out spikier than she preferred.

She looked at the brush in her hand. It had been Hawke's once. *Stop thinking about Hawke.* So had the silver chain around her wrist. There were little reminders everywhere. And if she thought about Hawke, she remembered where Hawke was. And if Star remembered where Hawke was, she didn't feel like going on a date anymore.

Star shook her head and looked away from the mirror. She was a huge mess. She would be doing Lissa a favor by not going on a date with her.

It's not a date! She admonished herself. She had spent several days in bed with Malena. No way was she going on a date with someone else after that. She took up her phone and wallet and put them in her pocket. She'd never before had to remind herself so often that she wasn't looking for a relationship. She had everything she needed in her life already. A proper relationship would just be a bother.

Her phone beeped. It was the alarm she had put so she wouldn't be late. She threw one last look in the mirror. *At least I look nice.* She usually didn't act so vain, but she wanted Lissa to find her good looking. She was too tired to analyze what that meant.

"I'm not going to cancel on her at the last minute," Star said to no one. "I can do this. I *want* to do this."

She grabbed her phone and her wallet and headed out the door. Time to play it cool.

*

Lissa was waiting for her by the door downstairs. When Star saw her lithe form, sheepish smile, and little black dress, little butterflies fluttered around her belly and chest. *What am I doing?* Her mother's alcohol binges and behavior had driven her out before. To bars. Into women's beds. Not on a date with a young woman who wasn't even her type. *This isn't a date.*

My body certainly doesn't know she isn't my type and that this isn't a date, Star thought as she greeted Lissa with a hug. She didn't want to let go. She pushed her face into Lissa's hair and inhaled deeply. The scent of her, something sweet and crisp, made Star want to forget about the dinner and the movie and hop straight into other nighttime activities. But this was Lissa. And Star had to tread lightly.

We're still just friends, remember?

It was harder and harder to remember that as the night progressed. Lissa acted completely normal and every single smile, every word, every gesture just made Star like her more.

"How was your week?" Star asked once they had ordered their food at Lissa's favorite Moroccan place. Anything to distract herself from that damned dimple in Lissa's left cheek. "Not too many demanding customers, I hope."

"It's okay." Lissa said. "Not going to lie though. I only think it's been okay because I've had this to look forward to."

"Same." Star didn't mind saying it, it was the truth.

"Really?" Lissa's face shone and she bit her lip. "That makes me kind of happy."

Fuck. Lissa was so cute she should have come with a warning. Fear gripped at Star's throat. It was paramount that Lissa didn't think this was a date. Star couldn't be strong for the both of them. She did the only thing she could think of.

"I spent some time with Malena though. It was nice."

Lissa's mouth formed a small *oh* and she looked down. It didn't bring Star any pleasure, but it had to be done, even though she could hardly remember why anymore.

"Why isn't she your girlfriend?" Lissa's tone had changed, but her gaze was still friendly. "Not to be like that, but you sleep together, right?" At the mentioning of 'sleep together,' Lissa turned a bit red but her facial expression didn't change.

Their food arrived and Star felt her stomach grumble. She hadn't eaten a proper meal yet that day, and as suspicious she had been when Lissa suggested Moroccan food, the plate that was placed in front of her smelled amazing. Star hurried to take a bite before answering.

"We are close friends. Have been all our lives. Sleeping together is like a habit for us." She grinned. "And we're good at it. But we don't love each other that way. That's how simple it is."

Lissa didn't answer that. She scooped up some rice and shoved it into her mouth, chewing thoroughly.

"When I wasn't with Malena," Star sighed. "I was with my mom. She's... ill."

*

"Oh." Lissa's heart fell. "I hope it isn't serious?"

"It is, kind of." Star leaned back on her chair. "So you watched any more of my stuff?"

Lissa's eyebrows knitted and, instead of feeling mortified, she just felt concerned. Star was deflecting and going the only route she knew how. Lissa wasn't going to push the subject of Star's ill mother, they hadn't known each other for that long. She decided to go along with it.

"Maybe." She held Star's gaze in defiance. "But I'll never tell."

Star chuckled.

"We both know what that means."

They finished their meals on a light note and walked together out of the restaurant. It really did feel like a date. Sure, none of them had brought the other flowers, but Lissa was wearing her little black dress and had curled her hair and even applied some make-up. She felt pretty and Star looked equally delicious in her black slacks and burgundy shirt.

Lissa looked at Star. She decided to take a chance. "Want to go back to my place and continue our quest to get our cows to pasture?"

Star grinned widely.

"Sure! Sounds fun."

They jumped on one of the busses that went by Lissa's home. It had started to drizzle and Star was visibly shivering.

"You can borrow a sweater when we get there."

"What? Oh." Star ran her hands over her arms in an attempt to warm herself. "Yeah, thanks."

She seemed a bit distracted. Lissa didn't like it.

They got off the bus and walked upstairs to Lissa's apartment. She let them in and thanked her lucky stars that she had actually tidied that very same morning.

"Want something to drink?"

They took off their shoes and Star went to sit down on her sofa. The action amused Lissa and warmed her heart in the same time. Star really acted at home in her little place. It felt normal. Like that was how it was supposed to be.

"Maybe something warm?" Star was starting to look pale.

"Are you getting ill?" Lissa couldn't ignore her concern anymore.

"No." Star leaned her head back on the sofa. "It was just a difficult week."

"Do you want to talk about it?"

Lissa turned her back to her as she put the kettle on, wanting to give Star some privacy.

"No. Not really."

When Lissa looked back around, Star was looking at her, a tired expression in her face. Her mouth was still smiling, but it didn't quite reach her eyes.

"Would you rather just go home?" Lissa prepared a pot of tea and grabbed two cups.

"No."

Okay, then.

She carried the pot and the two cups to the table and put them down.

"Sorry." Star shook her head. "I don't mean to ruin your evening."

"Don't be silly." Lissa got the game as well and sat down on the carpet next to Star, who was on the sofa, and started opening the box and setting it up. "I'm just sorry you're feeling so… umm… melancholic."

Star chuckled gently at her word choice.

"So where we?" She grabbed her cue and her cow. "I was here, wasn't I?"

Lissa nodded and grabbed hers and put it two steps behind Star's.

"You go first." She handed the dice to Star.

Star rolled it, moved her cue, and landed on an action card. She picked it up and read it in silence.

"You forgot to mix the deck," she said without looking up.

"Why?" Lissa stood up on her knees, put one hand on the sofa next to Star's thigh, and leaned in to look at the card that Star was holding.

It was the kissing noodle card. *Oh.*

Lissa turned her head, their gazes met. Lissa couldn't hear anything. Not the traffic. Her heart stopped. Time stopped. Everything went still as they stared at each other. Questions. Answers. Nothingness. Everything.

Time sped up again as Star threw the card to the side, put one of her arms around Lissa's shoulders, her other hand cradling her jaw and pulled her closer.

Finally.

Star's lips were firm and guided Lissa's in the kiss. It was so good, but as their lips danced, so did their bodies. Lissa's brain short-circuited as Star's hands were everywhere; travelling over her back and clutching at her ass as she pulled Lissa up on the sofa. Before Lissa knew what was happening, Star was on her back, with Lissa lying on top of her.

I... don't... know... what... to... do. The feelings were overpowering her. All she could do was cling to the collar of Star's shirt and keep kissing her, open-mouthed. She was drowning.

"Lissa." Her name felt like a prayer coming from Star's lips.

She claimed Star's lips again and whimpered when Star moved her hand from Lissa's back to her front and firmly pressed her hand to Lissa's breast.

Lissa felt her nipples harden against Star's palm, and she squirmed on top of Star's so very solid body. Her heart was beating so hard, in tandem with Star's, and instead of igniting her, Lissa felt a trickle of fear. She couldn't do this. She couldn't.

"Star." She tore her mouth from hers. "I'm sorry. I can't." She felt like crying. Her whole body pounded, but she didn't know if it was from panic or arousal.

"Shh…" Star pressed a kiss to her forehead and her touches turned gentle instead of hungry. "Hey? We don't have to do anything. Take it easy. You're okay, you're okay."

She let Lissa slip to her side so that they lay side by side, their bodies facing each other. But Lissa didn't look at her face, instead she burrowed her face in Star's neck, not saying anything. She just breathed, her hot breath hitting Star's skin.

"You're okay," Star repeated.

She kept one arm around Lissa's shoulders, keeping her close. The other she ran over Lissa's back up and down, soothing her.

This is ridiculous, Lissa thought, *I'm the one who's supposed to comfort her. She's the one who was having a bad week. Not me.*

But she didn't tell Star to stop. Not even as she felt herself drifting to sleep. Lissa couldn't remember ever feeling so content or safe. Or cared for.

*

It was already light when Star came to. At first she wasn't sure where she was or who she was holding on to, but as soon as she heard Lissa's quiet breathing, she knew exactly where she was. And she felt completely at home. Which meant she had to leave.

The situation was absurd. Their friendship was supposed to be just that: a friendship. A friendship like one that Star hadn't had before. She looked down and smiled. *Lissa.*

Star let herself press a kiss on top of honey-brown tresses. Lissa mumbled something and hugged Star closer.

"Are you awake?" Star whispered.

"Barely." Lissa sounded sleepy. "Did we sleep all night?"

"Seems like."

Lissa pulled away a bit so she could look at Star's face. Lissa looked worried and she bit her lip. Star was about to ask what was wrong when she opened her mouth.

"I'm not sexy like that, you know."

Lissa's words were so surprising that Star just snorted.

"What?" She rubbed Lissa's back again. "Where is this coming from?"

Lissa disentangled herself and they both sat up. She rubbed her knuckles into her eyes and then looked at Star. She looked weary.

"What's wrong?" Star wondered what was going on in her young friend's head.

"I just…" Lissa sighed. "I'm not sexy like some of the women you've been with. I'm not sure…. I… if… I can't do the things you…." She sucked in air through her mouth.

"Take it easy." Star patted her thigh. "You have nothing to worry about, okay? We're just friends, remember?"

Star smiled when Lissa nodded like a well-trained puppy.

"Good," she continued. "And I like really like being friends with you. There is nothing else we need to worry about right now. Sometimes friends accidently make out. Trust me, it's happened before."

Lissa raised an eyebrow and shook her head.

"Somehow, I don't believe that." She sighed. "You don't get it." She eventually whispered. There was a runaway look in her eyes that made Star worried.

"What is it? Please talk with me."

Lissa's eyes were wide, her pupils wide.

"I've never… I mean, I… fuck it. I'm a virgin."

She looked absolutely petrified and for one long moment, Star shared her fear. She had of course realized that Lissa wasn't the most experienced, but for her to have *never* had sex… *I definitely didn't see that coming.*

"How come?" Star asked eventually. "Not that there's anything wrong with it. But… you're…"

How young did she say she was? Star knew that Lissa had mentioned her age but right at this moment couldn't remember. She was over 18, right? Over 21?

"It's not like the situation didn't present itself." Lissa bit her bottom lip again. "I just haven't been that interested, and now it feels like it's grown out of proportion."

I'm so not the right person for her. Star didn't want Lissa to get the wrong idea about sex and she felt bad for pushing her to watching porn. *I'm such a jerk.*

"Stop it." Lissa's voice had gotten an edge to it.

"Huh?" Star looked up.

"You don't need to feel like you've corrupted me in any way. Or feel bad about things you've said to me." Lissa locked her arms in front of her chest. "Or feel bad about the way you kissed me. I'm a big girl. Period." She looked like she had relaxed a bit. "I've just…"

"I don't expect anything, Lissa." *How did I get in this conversation?* "Whatever it is that you've seen… it's my job. I receive instructions, I follow them through."

"But you like what you do."

"Yes, I do. If it's something I don't like, I won't do it."

They stared at each other. Lissa looked like she wanted to say something, but stayed quiet.

"I don't know what it is that you want me to say." Star felt like kicking the sofa.

"Me neither." Lissa sounded sad. "Want to forget about this? We're just friends anyway."

Star scratched her head and felt the tension leave her shoulders. *Brushing things off and avoiding them instead of dealing? A woman after my own heart.*

"Sure."

CHAPTER TWELVE

Malena's hand fisted Star's hair and pulled. The action was familiar and comforting. The sting made Star smile against Malena's naked breast.

"Why are you here?" The hold on her hair tightened. "You basically jumped me the moment I let you through the door."

"Mmm." Star pulled Malena's nipple between her lips and tugged with a hint of teeth. She let go. "I didn't have anything to say. I knew what I wanted."

Malena let go of her harsher grip and instead caressed.

"Star." She sounded hesitant.

"What?"

"I know I was gone for a while, but you've never needed me this much before." Malena chuckled. "I thought you had other—what should I call them—*friends*?"

"I do, but…" Star sat up and hugged her knees, the sheet pooling at her waist.

Malena scratched her nails over Star's back.

"What's wrong?"

Star couldn't answer. She couldn't tell Malena the truth. *I'm terrified I'm starting to like a woman. A normal woman I'm wrong for. I need you to make me forget her.*

"It's nothing."

"So it's not about your mom?"

Star shook her head.

"So, how about that girl? What was her name? Lissa?"

Star twitched and turned around, looking at Malena.

"Why would you say that?"

"Well..." Malena tilted her head to the side and stroked her hand over Star's back. "Relax, I'm not out to get you, stop tensing."

Star hadn't even known she was. She tried to relax her muscles and opened her clenched fists.

"Why would you say that?" She repeated but in a softer tone.

"Because you went home with her a few weeks ago, don't think I didn't notice. And when I called Deirdre a few days ago she said you were on a date. I thought maybe it was with her."

"It was with her." Star sighed. "But it wasn't a date. We just had dinner and afterwards we went to her place to play board games. She's becoming a dear friend but that's it." Star didn't know if she was lying to herself or to Malena. "She's fun to be around. I could use a sex-free friendship." She smiled, genuinely this time. "She actually messaged me a few hours ago inviting me to her sister's beach party."

"Beach party?" Malena laughed. "What is she? Sixteen?"

"No. Well, I think the sister is slightly younger, but they are both over twenty."

Malena regarded her for a while, silent.

"What?" Star eventually had to ask.

"I'm happy you have a new friend." Malena squeezed her shoulder. "It sounds like you needed her."

Yes, Star thought. *Seems like I really did.*

CHAPTER THIRTEEN

"Good thing I brought a spare, huh?" Dea handed Lissa a pale blue bikini, and for once, Lissa wholeheartedly agreed. She couldn't believe she had actually forgotten her swimming suit. She had packed it in the morning, put her bag by the door, and she had *still* forgotten it. The whole bag. It wasn't like her.

The happy shouts and splashes from outside beckoned her on as she wormed out of her sundress and panties and put Dea's bikini on. They were the same size, which was a relief. *I'm not in the mood to flash everyone today.* Not this crowd anyway.

"Ready?" Dea gathered her much longer hair into a ponytail just as Lissa let hers out. She wanted to feel the water pull at her hair. There was no freer feeling.

They joined hands and left the room, heading down the stairs. They had just crossed the threshold when Grayson swished past them, hitting Lissa's shoulder and breaking their contact. Dea shrieked like a pig, but ran willingly toward the water while Grayson laughed loudly. "Sorry, Liss."

"It's okay." She shook her head, smiling. *Crazy people.* She laughed.

"Should I do the same?" Turning around wasn't required, she knew who it was.

"You came!" Lissa turned around. Star was wearing a pair of shorts that looked two sizes too big and a white sport-style bikini. *When it gets wet it's going to be almost see-through.* It wasn't a completely unwelcome thought.

"Of course I came." Star grinned.

She coughed a bit and walked forward and offered her a hug.

Lissa's heart made a happy jump and hoped that Star didn't notice as she hugged her back.

"Hi."

"Hi."

They smiled at each other.

"Hi," a third person said.

"Oh." Lissa immediately let go of Star's waist. "Dea! This is Star, my new friend." She took a step back so that Dea and Star could shake hands. "This is Dea, my sister."

"Nice to meet you." Dea almost sounded like herself, but Lissa could hear it: the hesitation and mistrust. She almost wished she had never told Dea about Star's job. Star didn't the deserve the suspicion.

"Should we go out and swim?" Lissa felt nervous. Dea and Star were staring each other down as if deciding who was bigger.

Grayson chose that moment to stick his head out again.

"Come on, girls!"

Dea sighed and looked away from Star and to Grayson. The tension left the room.

"Sure, come on!"

They went through the house and out on the beach.

"Thanks for inviting me," Star said in a low voice to Lissa.

"It's no problem." Star was so close, it made Lissa feel unsettled, sick to her stomach. She was quite sure it could be relieved with a kiss though. "I wanted you here. I thought it would be fun. Not as fun as *The Crazy Cow Game* of course." She giggled. "But fun."

They got outside, and as soon as Star could see the water, her whole demeanor changed. She straightened her back and took a hold of Lissa's hand.

"Come on!" She pulled, starting to run.

Energy and happiness filled Lissa as they ran toward the sparkling blue. Her hair flowed behind her, her heart raced, the sun shone above. She threw herself in the water, hand in hand with Star. It was cold against her heated skin.

Their hands disengaged and she dove, needing to get used to the temperature. Goose bumps covered her body and she shuddered. She opened her eyes and looked at the kicking legs around her, the saltwater stinging. Right in front of her was Star with her eyes open too. They stared at each other.

*

Lissa's bikini looked amazing against her pale skin. She was covered in goose bumps, and Star almost felt guilty for pulling her into the water.

Sorry. She mouthed but only bubbles came out of her mouth.

Lissa shook her head and pointed upwards. Only then Star realized that her lungs were calling out for oxygen too. She pushed herself up, flowing through the water until her head broke the surface. She gasped for air.

"Why are you sorry?" Lissa appeared next to her. Drops of water dripped down her neck and between her breasts.

Star threw an arm over her own chest, suddenly feeling exposed. The feeling was foreign.

"You look cold." Star grimaced when someone else's foot kicked her in the shin. "I should have let you go into the water slowly."

"Don't worry about it." Lissa leaned backwards until she floated on her back. "I'll feel warm soon enough."

Star spotted movement in the corner of her eye and she held out her hand, catching the beach ball just before it hit Lissa's face.

"Sorry." Dea called out. "I thought we could play something."

"Okay." Lissa straightened up. "I'm in."

"Me too." Star chimed in; so did Grayson and a couple of people that Star didn't know. "Even if I don't know what we're playing."

"Just catch!" Dea threw it to the side.

"Me first!" Grayson went after it, crawling as fast as he could toward the ball that was bobbing on the waves. He got it and swam back to the group.

"Let's make this interesting, shall we?" He placed himself in the middle of the group. "Whoever gets it…" He bit her lip as if thinking deeply. "Oh hell, wins!" He threw it high into the air and then forward.

A thrill travelled down Star's spine. It wasn't a proper bet, and yet competitiveness claimed her soul. She dove under, convinced that she would be faster under the water than at the top. She kicked out with her feet and flew through the water. She didn't break the surface until she was right by the ball. She put her hand on it with a satisfied grin.

"I don't think so." Lissa grabbed it out of nowhere and kicked away from Star. She laughed loudly.

"No, you don't." Star dove forward, grabbed Lissa's ankle and pulled. Lissa yelled out and kicked with her other foot, hitting Star in the stomach but not hard.

Star wasn't thinking, she just wanted to win. She got Lissa's flailing legs and put them between her thighs. She squeezed, keeping them trapped. She put one arm around the ball and with the other *tickled* Lissa's stomach.

The reaction was immediate.

Lissa squealed, let go of the ball and tried to get Star to stop tickling her. This made her head go under the water, since she still couldn't use her legs. Star stared at the top of her head for two seconds before relaxing her legs and grabbing a hold of her waist with the arm not holding the ball.

Lissa coughed when Star helped her above the water.

"Oops." But Star couldn't help but smirk at the ball under her arm. At least she had won. She tried to ignore the quickening of her breath and heartbeat. Her whole body felt tense. Like when she was going to shoot a movie. Or when she was cruising in a club. Lissa's skin was so *soft*. It made Star remember the make out session just a week ago.

"You want to win so badly you almost drown me?" Lissa spluttered, but there was a gleam in her eyes, and the way she pinched Star's side let Star know that she was okay.

"Of course." Star winked at her and Lissa pinched her side again.

"You idiot." But the words were said with a smile.

*

Even though it was a beach party with no one she knew except Lissa, Star was having a great time. She had stayed in the background since they had got out of the water, sipping on her lemonade and looking at Lissa, who was talking to some other women. Thrills went through her when Lissa laughed. She looked so alive and beautiful it made Star ache inside.

Lissa looked at her. Their eyes met and Star hurried to look away. She chuckled to herself, not sure if she didn't like that Lissa had noticed that she was looking. She couldn't deny her cheeks growing a bit warm.

"Are you having fun?" Lissa came closer. "I'm sorry for leaving you alone, I just had to talk to Sanna and Sara a bit, I haven't seen them in ages."

"Don't worry." Star smiled. "I'm glad you're having a good time. It's nice to see you at a party you didn't plan."

Lissa went to her side and leaned against the same table. They looked out over the beach and the glittering sea.

"Me too."

She looked thoughtful for a while. Star was about to ask what it was when Dea came walking.

"What are you guys up to?"

"We're just talking," Lissa said.

"That sounds almost as boring as watching Grayson hit on every female thing here." She sounded grumpy.

Star and Lissa shared a look. The edge of Lissa's lip curled into an amused smile. Realization hit Star.

"Sometimes young men are quite oblivious." Lissa leaned her head on Dea's shoulder. "Maybe you should just—"

"Just what?" Dea whined and pulled away. "And what do you know about young men?" She folded her arms in front of her chest, the look in her face screaming annoyance. "Lesbians," she muttered under her breath. Then she looked at Star. "What about you?"

"What about me?" Star regarded the sisters.

Dea looked hilarious, like an angry kitten. Her eyes were tiny slits and her mouth a frown, but she looked so cute and young that she didn't look intimidating at all. Star didn't know how old Dea was but guessed that as the baby of the family, she was probably a little bit immature.

"You're like Lissa, aren't you? Or are you able to actually give me advice on men?"

"Dea!" Lissa sounded shocked and appalled at Dea's frank tone, but Star just burst out laughing.

"If you mean the lesbian thing, yeah, I'm like Lissa." Star chuckled. "But I still think it's sound advice. Trust me, I grew up with three little cousins who were more like brothers, each more oblivious to what was right in front of them. Sometimes you just got to grab them by the—" the women stared at her. "—eh, the tie. Make them notice you."

Dea groaned and covered her face with her hands.

"I don't even want him for myself, I just don't want anyone else to have him. Is that so bad?"

"Yeah, kinda." Star smiled at her gently, very aware of Lissa's gaze burning into the top of her head. "How long have you been friends?"

Dea didn't answer but just groaned again.

"They've been friends for as long as either of them can remember," Lissa filled in. "They were in the same kindergarten class. Then different schools but took field hockey together, then the same high school. Then applied for the same college. Now they're both in med school."

"I'm not even sure I like him." Dea blurted out. "I mean, I get jealous, but that doesn't mean anything, does it?"

She looked at Star purposely, as if really expecting an answer. Clearly she didn't share her sister's subtlety and sense of privacy. Lissa, on the other hand, had started looking a bit pale. Her smile was strained.

"Dea, maybe you should ask one of your little girlfriends and not someone you don't know. Star is here to enjoy herself, not—"

"Please, I don't mind," Star hurried to say. "But I don't have an answer for you." She looked at Dea. "Only you know what you're feeling. And I'm not exactly a good person to come to for that kind of advice."

"Are all lesbians this hopeless?" Something gleamed in Dea's eyes when she looked at Star. It made Star wonder how much she knew. How much had Lissa told her? About their friendship? About their kisses?

"Oh, God." Lissa rolled her eyes. "Go and bother someone else." She gave Dea a push but Dea refused to move.

"Are you an exhibitionist?"

"Dea!" Lissa exclaimed.

Star's eyes went wide. So Dea knew, right? She had to, why would she otherwise ask that?

"A little, I guess." Star decided to answer. "I have to be to enjoy what I do."

"So you really are a porn star then?"

"Don't talk so loudly!" Lissa hissed.

Star threw her a look, her heart falling. Was Lissa still embarrassed over porn? Even now that they were friends?

"I don't mind," she said. "Ask what you need to ask."

"How long have you been doing it?" Dea folded her arms over her chest.

"A good four years now," Star said. "But not all year around, I have periods when I do more and periods I do less."

"Stop questioning her." Lissa poked Dea in the ribs and had to pull her away again. "She doesn't have to answer to you."

"Well, she does if she's going to date my sister," Dea hissed back.

"Now, wait a minute." Star had had enough. "Lissa and I aren't dating. We're just friends. And even if we were dating, I still don't have to defend my job to you."

Dea sucked in air through her nose.

"Fine," she said in a calmer voice. "I guess I don't. Sorry, I just… protective instincts kicking in and all that."

"Don't worry," Star said. "I'd never do anything to hurt Lissa." *I'll never give myself opportunity to do so.*

Dea and Lissa shared a look. Lissa looked so furious and mortified at the same time that Star almost felt sorry for her.

"Fine, I'll go." Dea straightened up. "I need to find Grayson anyway. Hey, I'm sorry if I made you feel uncomfortable or anything."

"Don't mention it." But Star couldn't deny that she relaxed a bit when Dea left them alone again.

"I'm sorry," Lissa whispered.

*

Lissa felt mortified. This was supposed to be a calm and fun outing for her to enjoy with Star, and instead Dea had ruined it with her stupid questions.

"You have nothing to be sorry for." Star shrugged. "It's normal to be protective of your siblings. Are you much older? Sometimes the youngest continue being young for the longest time. My youngest cousin still acts like a baby sometimes, and he's almost thirty."

Lissa raised one of her eyebrows.

"I'm the younger one."

"Oh! Sorry, I just assumed..." Star's eyes went wide and she spoke hurriedly. "Not because you look older, it was more based on behavior. I..."

"Relax!" A laugh escaped her. "We're more like twins than anything, less than two years between us." In fact, Lissa had been born just 13 months after Dea. They were in different school years, but otherwise they were more like twins. Triplets, if you counted Grayson.

"Oh." Star bit her lip. She chuckled nervously. "I don't know what to say now." When she smiled, a dimple appeared in one of her cheeks. "Did you tell her about me?"

The answer was obvious and Lissa didn't even try to deny it.

"I did." She fought every instinct to hold Star's hand that was close to hers. "I told her you were a new friend and that—" She inhaled and gathered bravery "—that I like you a little."

Instead of happiness she noticed dread filling Star's eyes. *What happened? What did I do?*

"Lissa." Star sounded a bit breathless. "We're just friends. I know we kissed and everything but... that's all there will be between us."

Lissa's mouth dried up and she blinked her eyes a couple of times. She felt like an idiot.

"Of course. I'm sorry." *I'm so stupid. Why did I think she would like me?*

"Don't be sorry!" Star reached out but Lissa took a step back. Her eyes were filled with a sympathy that made Lissa feel nauseous. *So, this is what rejection feels like.* "Please, Lissa."

"Don't worry." Her voice was shaky but she managed to keep the tears back. "I'll be okay." She looked up again and smiled, hoping it didn't look too forced. *Is it because I'm a virgin?*

"You better be." Star's smile was teasing, but her eyes still looked worried. "We can't stop being friends now, our cows haven't managed to pasture yet."

"Yeah." Lissa's laugh sounded disingenuous even to her own ears. *Is it because I'm not her type?*

"Do you want to swim again?"

"No." Lissa inhaled slowly and exhaled. She was good at this, pushing her feelings away. Faking normalcy until she felt normal again. "I'm a little bit cold actually."

"We can go if you want," Star said. "But Lissa?" Star grabbed a hold of her arm. Her touch was so sweet, it only amplified Lissa's inner turmoil.

"What?"

"Friends?"

Lissa nodded.

"Friends."

CHAPTER FOURTEEN

"Yes, ma'am, I understand." Lissa sighed, closed her eyes, and held the phone away from her ear as Mrs. Ramsey, the client with the twin birthday party, yelled at her.

"No, ma'am, but that's not—" *Remain professional, remain professional.* Lissa couldn't stand somebody yelling at her and was doing everything she could not to burst into tears. She wasn't sad or scared, or taking it personally, but the uncomfortableness of it all made her shake inside.

"And don't even get me started on the cake!" Mrs. Ramsey's tone had turned shrill.

Lissa worked against the instinct to defend herself. Whatever Ramsey was upset about, it wasn't her. Or the party. It was probably something else. Some personal issues that she was taking out on Lissa. It wasn't the first time.

"Mrs. Ramsey, maybe it would be better if you talked with my supervisor, Yolanda Powell." *It's not my freaking job to listen to this.*

Mrs. Ramsey drew in a breath that seemed to last for several minutes.

"Fine." Her tone was still snappy, but she had stopped yelling. "Give me her number, then!"

Lissa gave her Yolanda's number and then she was finally able to turn off the call.

She sunk back into her chair with a relieved sigh, glad the call was over.

I really need to find another job.

*

Star ignored Malena's question and slipped another quarter into the laundry machine.

"Star?"

Why did I invite Malena for a laundry-date? Star should have known that Malena would have been insistent on talking about stupid, important stuff.

"Yes?"

"How have you been? It's been a while since you came over now."

"Good." It was a standard answer. But when she thought of it, it was actually an honest one too. A lot of parts of her life sucked, but because of Lissa, she felt okay anyway. Good even. For the past week they had talked almost every night on the phone, and once met to squeeze in some *Crazy Cow* time.

"Why did you just smile?" Malena had a puzzled look in her face. "We're inside a laundromat, the least happy place on earth. What's up?"

Star bit her lip hard while thinking.

"I wasn't smiling." She smiled again and threw up her hands. "Fine. I met someone."

"I knew it!" Malena grabbed her hand and looked at her with an open mouth. "Finally. The cute, little thing, right?"

Little thing? Star felt a bit queasy at that description. *Is that how we usually talk about women?*

"Yes. That's her."

"I wish I was surprised. But she's so tiny!" Malena seemed more surprised than anything. "And young. Are you sure?"

"Yeah, I'm sure. She's different. But funny. And sexy." She felt herself blush. The second time in God knows how long. "We're totally wrong for each other though. I mean, I'm totally wrong for her anyway."

"Why?"

Star sighed and pulled her fingers through her hair, it was getting too long.

"I don't know," she said eventually. "She likes me, she told me even."

"That's brave of her. What did you answer?"

"I told her we're just friends."

Malena grabbed her shoulder.

"You rejected her even though you like her too?"

"No." Star bit her lip. "Yes, maybe. I don't know."

"Star." Malena waited until Star looked at her. "You've never even mentioned a woman to me, not in this way. You must really like her."

Star wanted to argue but couldn't. Just thinking about Lissa made her warm inside. She looked around before leaning in and talking in a low voice.

"She's a virgin."

"So?" Malena shrugged. "Sex isn't everything, no matter what you think. If you really like her, you'll figure it out together."

It was nice to hear Malena say that, even though Star wasn't sure it was that simple.

*

"Hello, Hawke." Star walked over to the right side of the bed. The side that her mom's unseeing eyes were turned towards. "How are you doing?"

After the laundry was done and she'd said bye to Malena, Star had decided to visit Hawke. Her mother was still in the hospital and less verbal than ever. Star didn't think Hawke could even see her anymore. But something had still pulled her back to the hospital. To her mother.

She knows I'm here, right? Star needed to believe that.

"The doctor says your condition hasn't changed." She stroked strands of hair off of Hawke's forehead. "Are you gonna die on me?"

Hawke had no answers for her.

"I met a girl, Mom." Star sat down next to her. "You'd hate her. Not a big drinker. No drugs. Careful. And definitely not sexually liberated." *And I've already fallen for her, hard. How pathetic am I?* "And your daughter is slowly but surely being lured away from the wide path of depravity. You really wouldn't approve."

Star couldn't help to remember the never-ending parade of men and women her mom had brought home over the years. The parties. How old had Star been the first time her mother smoked pot around her? Probably less than five. She'd never even had a chance to be normal. Anger rose within her and she forced air out of her lungs.

"Miss Ciel?" There was a nurse in the doorway. "Visiting hours are almost over."

"That's fine." Star got up. "I was done here anyway." Before she left, she took a deep breath and forced herself to calm down. She wouldn't leave in anger. "See you soon, Mom." She brushed a few more hairs off of Hawke's forehead.

CHAPTER FIFTEEN

Star found herself outside Lissa's door the same afternoon. She knocked, her heart beating fast while she waited for it to open. It did after almost five minutes. Lissa must have been in the shower because her hair was wet and her clothes looked thrown on, her shirt twisted to the side, showing off a white bra-strap with blue flowers on.

"Hi."

"Hi?" Lissa turned her head to the side. "Star? What are you doing here? Come in!"

"No, I was wondering if you wanted to take a walk," Star said. "I need some fresh air."

"Sure." Lissa nodded. "I just need to grab my purse and my coat, give me a second."

*

They walked through the local park, stopped by a pond and regarded the ducks swimming there. Star hadn't said a word during the entire time, and even though Lissa didn't push her, it was puzzling. *Maybe something at work? Something with her mom?* Lissa was sure Star would start talking when she was ready.

Lissa looked at the ducks. It was going towards Fall, and it was a particular cold day.

"I wish we had brought some bread." Lissa wanted to feed them.

"They're allergic to bread," Star said. "It's better to feed them corn, peas, or certain types of seeds."

Lissa raised an eyebrow.

"My hippie mother made sure that everyone knew how dangerous most humans were to animals. She told me about that duck thing probably ten times before I turned six."

Lissa reached out and squeezed her hand.

"I'm sorry she's ill."

"I'm not. Come on." Star tugged on her arm and pulled her to a nearby bench.

They sat down.

"I went to see her before this. She's not talking at all anymore."

"Oh." Lissa didn't know what to say.

"I hope you don't think badly of me for talking about it this way."

Lissa ran her hand across Star's back, needing to touch her. She followed the curve of Star's shoulders.

"I don't know anything about you and your mom," she said. "There's nothing for me to judge."

"She's used drugs all my life, before I was born too. The drugs caused her to have a stroke before I was fifteen. Since then she hasn't been… normal."

"Oh." Lissa didn't know what to say. "I can't imagine growing up with a drug-addicted mother." Even though Lissa's parents had left her early, they'd always been loving and quite perfect.

"Huh." Star looked bitter. "She was addicted when I was born already. It's given me problems all my life."

"How come?"

Star felt so tense that Lissa almost felt scared. But something drove her to keep talking, maybe Star needed to tell. She flattened her palm so she could touch Star with a bigger surface and placed her arm around her waist.

"Do you know what neonatal abstinence syndrome is?"

"No." Lissa didn't want to know. It didn't seem like something nice.

"It's when a baby is born already addicted." She sighed. "Since I was exposed to drugs already in the womb, I was born craving and in withdrawal. I was also born premature and pretty sick, had seizures and high fevers."

Lissa's eyes widened. She felt like her heart stopped.

"But you're okay, right? Now?"

"I'm okay. Sure, I was diagnosed failure to thrive, and in spite of tall parents, I've remained quite short even as an adult. But I'm okay."

Lissa felt like her heart was breaking. *Oh, Star.*

"And you know what the funniest thing is?" Star laughed mirthlessly. "A couple of weeks ago, she somehow got hold of a bottle of whisky and swallowed pills. Had to be rushed to the hospital."

Lissa stayed silent. She didn't know what to say.

"I'm sorry. I've ruined your day." Star looked up at Lissa now. Her face looked blank, no emotions peeking through. "I shouldn't have come to you. I didn't even come to tell you this."

"Why did you come?" *She must feel awfully vulnerable after telling me all that.* Lissa kept her voice light and rubbed over Star's back. Star didn't answer. She wanted to lighten up the mood somehow. "So, I'm a virgin." It immediately had the effect she had hoped.

Star burst out laughing. She laughed until tears fell from her eyes.

"Oh God, Lissa. Thanks for that."

"I'm just glad I could make you smile again." Lissa bumped their shoulders together. "Come on, let's go back home. I'm expecting a phone call, and I left my work phone at home, but we can go out for dinner after if you'd like."

"You know what?" Star smiled at her. "That sounds great."

They walked back to Lissa's place, neither of them talking. Lissa didn't know what to say, and Star's gaze was distant, not looking at Lissa and saying nothing.

When they got up to her apartment again, Star sat down on the sofa like she owned the place, took out her phone, and looked at it. Lissa shrugged and got her laptop out. It was Saturday, but she still needed to check for emails and double-check her calendar.

She glanced at Star, who was still immersed in stuff on her phone. *It must be her way to escape. Maybe it would be better to let her go home and deal with whatever it is that is eating her.*

"I have to make a quick call." The people still hadn't called, and Lissa had to check why.

Star nodded without looking up.

Fine then. Lissa sighed and grabbed her phone. But instead of unlocking it, she just stared at it.

"You know what?" She couldn't keep the annoyed tone out of her voice. "If you're gonna be like that you might as well go home."

Star lifted her head then, and her wide eyes and open mouth immediately made Lissa feel guilty. *What is wrong with you? She needs comforting now, not...* Star looked utterly surprised.

"I'm sorry." Star got up and started walking toward the door. "I'll go."

"No!" Lissa hurried forward, grabbed Star's hand, and pulled her to a halt.

"What is it?" Star averted her gaze, her face slightly flushed and her mouth so far from a smile that it made Lissa's heart pound in something resembling fear.

"Don't go," Lissa whispered. "I'm sorry, I shouldn't have gotten annoyed with you."

Then she did the only thing she could think of, she took a firm hold on the back of Star's neck and pressed their lips together. Star produced a surprised whimper, but there was no resistance in her actions. Her hands came to rest around Lissa's waist and she turned her head to deepen their kiss. Lissa felt like her muscles were melting as she opened her mouth and granted access to Star's tongue.

In that moment, there was no hesitation. In that kiss, Lissa knew that Star liked her back. She had to.

She felt her legs walking forward as she secured Star against the wall. She felt Star grin against her lips, and she moved her head back to take a proper look at her.

Star's lips were slightly open and red, her face flushed, but the sad look in her eyes was gone. Lissa couldn't believe that she was holding Star against the wall. *What's happening to me?*

"Do you know what you're doing to me?" Star's mouth crooked. She undulated her hips against Lissa's. It didn't matter who was holding who against the wall. Star was still in control.

"No. Yes." Lissa swallowed. "It seems like my body has more of an idea than I do."

"I am not complaining." Star sounded deliciously breathless before she leaned forward and claimed Lissa's lips again. "Do you know why I came here today?"

"Why?"

"To do this. To tell you that I want to date you. Properly."

Happiness filled Lissa's being. *Oh Star, Star, Star, Star.*

*

Star's body was on fire. She clutched her hands around Lissa's perfect ass and pulled her closer. As much as she liked kissing, she needed more, more of Lissa, and she abandoned her mouth to nibble down her neck.

"Star." Lissa's breathless voice caused ripples of excitement to pulse through Star.

"What is it?" Star was almost embarrassed at how raspy her voice sounded. She was a professional after all, she was used to being in control of her emotions, but right now Lissa was making it hard to think.

She was so wet, all she wanted to do was grab Lissa's hand and push it where she needed it. Or guide Lissa's mouth lower.

But Lissa's inexperience demanded something different of Star. Star couldn't just take her pleasure like she was used to. It felt like all the usual rules were all thrown out of the window.

"I've dreamt of you." Lissa's eyes were closed and she was gasping as if drowning. "I've dreamt about you touching me, holding me. Making me ache inside." The familiar adorable blush spread over her cheeks and bridge of her nose. "You've already made me come twice in the past week." She bit her lip.

Star was completely speechless. What could she possibly reply to that? Anything she could say would lack in magnitude to what she was feeling.

To hear that Lissa had already come because of *her* made her weak in the knees. And just about ready to come herself.

She grabbed a firmer hold of Lissa's hips and pulled their pelvises together.

"I need you to be sure." She didn't feel the need to explain what she meant. "Please." The embarrassing word slipped out before she could stop it.

Lissa opened her eyes; her pupils so large her eyes looked black.

"What if I can't please you?"

The silly question almost made Star laugh again.

"Don't worry about that." She pulled her fingers through Lissa's hair. "Just let me touch you, okay?"

Lissa nodded. "Okay." Her voice was so small it made Star want to hold her.

As she turned around and led Star to her bed in the corner of the room, her chest was rising and falling so quickly that Star almost felt bad. She didn't want to push Lissa into something she wasn't comfortable with. She didn't want her *panicked.*

"We don't need to do this, you know?" *We are just friends, right?* Then again, Star slept with Malena too.

Lissa looked at her as she wordlessly took off her T-shirt. She wasn't wearing anything underneath, and her pink-tipped breasts grabbed Star's attention from the start.

Her mouth watered.

"I know we don't have to do this." Lissa's words brought Star's attention back to her face. "But I want to. Even if I'm terrified." She giggled.

Gosh, you're so adorable you should come with a warning. Star opened the buttons of her shirt but didn't remove it completely.

"Come here." She grabbed a hold of Lissa's hand and guided her to the bed.

She sat down on the bed and motioned for Lissa to straddle her lap. She kissed her young friend. Deeply. Thoroughly. While moving her hands on her back up and down. All she wanted to do was cradle Lissa's breast and pull her mouth to those delicious looking nipples, but she was also aware of Lissa's rapid breathing and whimpering, and she forced herself to go slow. The last thing she wanted was to scare Lissa.

Lissa sat on top of her thighs. They looked at each other, Lissa's arms around her neck, Star's hands on her slender waist. Star moved one of her hands from Lissa's middle to her thigh. The heat that was radiating from the juncture of Lissa's thighs was dizzying.

She pressed her fingers to the middle seam of Lissa's jeans.

"Oh." Lissa's forehead dropped down on Star's shoulder. "More of that, please."

Yes, ma'am. Star pressed a kiss to Lissa's cheek and palmed her. Lissa had started trembling, and the muscles in her legs were flexing, but she wasn't moving.

"You're killing me, you know that, right?" Star placed her mouth close to Lissa's ear. "You're so freaking sexy."

"Really?"

"Yes." Star nipped at her earlobe and smiled at the shiver that followed. "I want you completely naked, is that okay?

Lissa nodded, but when she leaned backward her shoulders were slumped, and she kept her arms crossed over her chest. There were goose bumps on her arms, and even though Star rubbed them, it didn't seem to get better.

"Are you cold?"

"No." Lissa still hadn't moved. "I'm just not used to getting completely naked with someone, you know? I'm feeling a little bit… exposed."

Their gazes met and Star's heart surged.

"I don't know how you did it."

"Did what?" Star pressed another kiss to her nose, unable to sit completely still. She needed to touch *her*.

"Got naked with so many other people."

Oh.

"This isn't really the time I want to think about that, is that okay?" Star didn't mind talking about it. But not here, not now. "We can talk about it some other time if you want."

Lissa nodded. She got up and took her pants off. She chewed on her bottom lip again but then took her underwear off too. Star stayed seated as she did, enjoying the view of Lissa's sculpted thighs and the small buzz of hair at the base of her stomach. She would have taken her pants off as well, but she didn't want any focus on herself or her own need.

"Come back up here." She patted her thigh.

Lissa rubbed her legs together and smiled sheepishly.

"I don't want to get your pants wet."

"You're crazy if you think I care about that."

This time Lissa did as asked. The bed dipped as she placed a knee in front of Star. Their hands met and Star pulled her forward but gently, not hurried, until Lissa was again placed against her. They kissed slowly, and while Lissa was all wrapped up in the kiss, Star placed one arm around Lissa's waist and put her other hand right against her. She was met with more wetness than she had anticipated and she groaned loudly.

"Oh, sweetheart."

Lissa cried out as Star stroked the slick skin under her fingers. *Mmmm, right there.* She swirled her fingers around her opening but didn't go inside. She wanted to, by God, she wanted to sink three fingers inside of her without a second thought. But she couldn't do that until she knew Lissa was ready.

*

Lissa pumped her hips against Star's searching fingers, all thoughts gone from her head. She didn't care that she was naked anymore, she didn't care about all the other people Star had slept with, or if her actions were wanton or inappropriate. All Lissa knew was Star's fingers, Star's lips, and Star's solid presence against her. Her inner muscles clenched around nothing as she ground herself firmer against Star. She knew what she wanted, she knew what she needed, but she didn't have words to ask for it. She just hoped that Star understood.

"Can I go—?" Star didn't even have to finish her choking sentence.

"Yes! Please, please, please, please, oh fuck." When Star actually entered her, Lissa didn't know what to do. Her throat closed up and she tilted her head backwards, certain that Star wouldn't let her fall.

To her surprise, Star did let her fall, but only to her back on the bed and she followed. When she was on her back, Star could thrust deeper, and Lissa was quickly learning that this was probably her favorite position so far. She arched her back and held her arms tight around Star's neck.

She knew what was coming, and yet she couldn't believe that this was actually happening. Somewhere in the back of her mind, she was aware of scratching at Star's back and the lewd sounds that were coming from her throat.

A slapping sound of skin hitting skin filled the little apartment and Star grunted. Of pleasure or exertion, Lissa didn't know, but she hoped it was the first. She wanted to give some back. She wanted Star to share what she was feeling. For both of them to fall over the edge together. But there was nothing Lissa could do.

As Star pulled out and came back with one more finger, Lissa had no choice. Before she knew what was happening, her muscles clenched around Star, and she opened her mouth in a silent scream. Every cell in her body came alive and with them, Lissa knew what life was. She felt like she had been frozen for years but now her body thawed and bloomed. All because of Star.

"Star." Lissa came down from her high and there was only one word left on her lips. "Star." It wasn't a shout but a soft, mumbled word.

"You okay?" Star was lying still on top of her, hand still firmly between her thighs.

"More than okay." For some reason Lissa felt her face heat and a sudden sadness well up in her chest. It was as if she had just experienced the most closeness she would ever experience with Star. And now that it was over, she *missed* her. Totally. Completely.

"I want to do that again."

Star looked up at her and grinned. She wiggled her fingers.

"Well, just give me a moment and I'll make you feel so good you won't be able to walk for the rest of the day."

Star's words were enough to curl Lissa's toes, but that wasn't what she wanted.

"No."

"No?" Star's voice changed tone and she lifted her head to get a better look at her.

Lissa winced as Star removed her hand.

"No, I want to. I want to make you feel good now. It's your turn. Or my turn, depending on how you look at it." Lissa rested her hands on top of Star's shoulders.

"You know you don't have to?" Star looked at her with honeyed eyes.

Oh, for the love of...

"Yes, I know I don't have to. Stop worrying." Lissa pushed on her until they sat up.

She took in Star's firm muscles and dark nipples and the divisions between her abs. She looked better than she did in her pictures and movies. Suddenly, it came back. All she had seen. And suddenly insecurity gripped at her again. Star had slept with so many people, Lissa didn't know how she could ever do anything to rock Star's world. She didn't want to be just one of many. She wanted to leave a permanent mark. Be someone special.

"What are you thinking about?" Star's hand came as if from nowhere and pulled through her head. The touch was comforting. "Whatever it is, don't."

"But—"

Star shifted onto her knees, pulled her zipper down. She grabbed a hold of Lissa's wrist and pulled her up too. Then she proceeded to push Lissa's hand down her pants.

"What are you—" Lissa's heart skipped a beat when she felt what Star wanted her to feel.

"Do you feel that?"

"Mhhmm."

Star was wet against her hand, wet and warm and all smooth silk. Lissa didn't know what to do at first, but she pressed forward with her fingers, eager to find Star's clit. When she did, she pressed down and Star shuddered.

"Yeah, just like that." Star's voice was several octaves lower than usual, and the sound of it sent shivers down Lissa's spine.

"Help me." Lissa didn't know what to do. *Should I go inside her? Like she did me? Should I touch her harder? Softer?*

"Don't worry." Star sounded strained. "You're doing fine. Just... keep... like... that." She grabbed a hold of Lissa's wrist and guided it back and forth so that Lissa's movement on her clit didn't stop.

Star was so wet, so slippery, that Lissa barely meant to go inside, but when she did, Star threw her head back and groaned gutturally.

"Another finger. Three, use three."

Lissa did as she was asked and almost as soon as she did, the muscles around her fingers started quivering. Star was almost swaying, and Lissa was starting to worry that she would fall. She put an arm around Star's shoulders to keep her upright. When she accidentally thrusted a bit harder than she meant, Star produced a whimpering female noise that Lissa recognized from her videos.

"Yeah, yeah, yeah... oh, fuck." She bucked her hips hard against Lissa's hand and then with a guttural cry, she came around Lissa's fingers.

And in that moment, Lissa knew that she had been wrong. She had been close to tears earlier, thinking that she would never be as close to another human being as with Star's fingers inside of her, but she had been wrong. That hadn't been it, this was. This was the moment she had been waiting for all her life. Giving Star pleasure made Lissa feel more powerful than she had ever felt before.

They had been on their knees the whole time, but now they fell on top of the covers.

"Mmm." Star ran her hands over Lissa's back.

Lissa's chest trembled, and it was only when Star laughed again that Lissa realized that she was practically purring like a cat. She removed her hand from inside Star's pants and flexed her fingers. Star grabbed her hand and wiped it on the top of her jeans, then she put it to her lips and kissed Lissa's knuckles.

"Was that as scary as you thought it would be?" Star pulled Lissa to her and placed her head on Lissa's chest. Her hand came to rest upon Lissa's breast.

"Scarier." Lissa ran her hand through Star's hair. "But totally worth it. I want to do it again."

"Do you now?" Star pressed a kiss to the skin underneath her mouth. "That's good news."

Lissa stretched her legs and arms. She did want to do it again, but she also wanted to eat something, to shower and to sleep. To cuddle. All at once.

"We need to eat something." She kept scratching her nails along Star's scalp.

"Mmm, sure... we will." Star yawned. "But a nap first, yes?"

"Take your pants off." Lissa wanted to see her. "And let's get under the covers." She yawned herself and felt her eyelids grow heavy.

Star kicked her jeans off and crawled under the covers. Her eyes were closed within a minute. Lissa hadn't even had a proper chance to look at her, she had just glanced at completely smooth skin. Star was completely shaved and she hoped that Star hadn't minded the fuzz between her own legs.

She yawned again and laid down next to Star under the cover. Her bed wasn't big, barely a twin, and it felt intimate to lie so close to her. Star was breathing calmly now, her eyelids slightly fluttering, and Lissa grabbed her hand. She knew she was falling asleep too, but she didn't want to feel far away from her while sleeping.

CHAPTER SIXTEEN

Mmmm. So soft. Star smiled against the soft skin under her cheek. With a satisfied feeling in her belly and a smile on her lips, she couldn't remember being this content in a long time. Even her usually troubled mind was calm. She ran her fingers over Lissa's ribs and giggled at the goose bumps that formed.

"Are you cold?" She whispered even though she knew the answer. Lissa had pulled the covers over them sometime during the afternoon, and Star couldn't just feel the sweat on her own skin but taste it on Lissa's. In the safety of their cocoon, no one could be cold.

Lissa put her arms around Star's neck and pulled her up so they were face to face. Slick skin over slick skin. Lissa shuddered again and Star held her closer. Her friend was trembling. *Be nice to her. Can you even remember your own first time? Okay, Star? No teasing!*

Star was lying on top of her now and Lissa's heart was beating so hard, Star could feel it. Even with them just lying there, Star couldn't remember ever feeling so close to another human being. Which was a funny feeling for a porn star. Or at least it should be, Star mused.

Lissa's face turned a lovely shade of pink as she slowly spread her thighs, giving Star room to lie between them. The look in Lissa's face, a mix of embarrassment and desperate arousal, sent shooting stars down Star's spine.

She rocked her hips. Halfway out of instinct, halfway out of need.

"Mmmm." Lissa put her hand on the back of Star's neck and pulled her down for a kiss. "This is nice."

Star moved above her. Slowly, gently, just keeping their fire stoked. Lissa closed her eyes and tipped her head backwards, and Star couldn't help but nip and lick at the soft neck under her lips.

"Don't mark me," Lissa mumbled. At first Star didn't know what she meant, but since she had sunk her teeth into Lissa's smooth neck, she figured it out soon enough.

"Sorry," she mumbled and licked the red mark.

"It's okay." Lissa put her arms around Star's waist and squeezed her. "I like it."

Star nipped at the skin again but then decided to do her best to not mark her. She wasn't a teenager; she could control herself. She ran her hands down Lissa's waist and cupped her ass, pulling her closer and rocking into her. Both of them were wet and their scents mingled. Star wanted to take her again and almost wished she was strapped, even though she knew that all of this was still new to Lissa. The thought of sinking into—

A phone rang loudly somewhere in the room. For one horrible moment, Star thought it was hers and that it was about Hawke. But it was Lissa's. They shared a look.

"Should I get off?"

"No." Lissa bit her lip. "Yes. I should probably take it." She stuck out her tongue. "But don't think I want to."

"I won't." Star rolled off her.

Lissa scrambled off the bed and walked toward her phone. Star laid on her side and appreciated Lissa's naked form.

She really is gorgeous. The slight dip in her back, the artistic spread of freckles on her back and butt, her messy hair. Star grinned when she thought about Lissa's messy hair and how it was because of her. She wanted to rock Lissa's world. She wanted to change her completely. *Get a grip, Star. Are you even dating?*

"Okay, fine. Bye." Lissa finished her call and turned off. She placed her phone on the dresser. She turned around again and looked at Star. As if her own nakedness suddenly dawned on her, she smiled nervously and placed an arm around her waist.

"Come here." Star didn't recognize her own voice. That dark note that she usually reserved for acting had come out on its own. Something inside her pounded, beckoned her to hold out her hand. She wanted Lissa. Needed her.

"Star."

"What?"

"Are we still just friends?"

"Oh."

Lissa took a step forward and sat down on the bed in front of her.

"Uh..." Star's head spun and goosebumps stood up. "No, I don't think so."

"How can you not know?" Lissa sounded annoyed.

"I think I need to eat something." Star scratched the back of her hair. "I can't think."

Lissa sighed but then nodded.

"We didn't eat last night." She leaned forward and pressed a kiss to Star's cheek. "But don't think I'm letting you off the hook. Is beans and toast fine?"

Star nodded, grateful for how cool Lissa was and that she hadn't pushed the issue. She watched as Lissa waltzed around the kitchenette, whistling, while taking out bread from the cupboard and pouring a tin of beans into a saucepan. Lissa hadn't gotten properly dressed, just pulled a big T-shirt over her head, but Star picked up her clothes from the floor and put them on.

*

Lissa's heart sang. There were no other words to better describe it. She watched the beans bubble as she listened to Star move around in the room behind her. A quiet hum of arousal still hummed through her, and the recent memory of skin on skin was more than enough to make her press her thighs together. Lissa felt like charcoal. Burned already but with the ability to set wood on fire.

"Smells good." Star placed her head on Lissa's shoulder. Their heights were perfect for it.

"It's just baked beans and tomato sauce, heated from a can." Lissa smiled. "But I guess when you feel hungry anything can smell good." She took the saucepan off the heat. "Can you put two slices of bread in the toaster? And I think I have some margarine in the fridge if you want."

While Star did as she was told, Lissa put the saucepan on the table and took out two plates and two glasses which she filled to the brim with water. *We better hydrate,* she thought with a grin.

Soon they were sitting at her little two-man table on her mismatched chairs.

"I don't know how you manage," Star said with a laugh, "to make beans taste like a gourmet meal."

"I want to say that the secret is in the sauce, but I think you're talking about something else. Plus, I almost burnt them."

Star grinned and ate a big scoop of beans. Lissa wanted to kiss the smile on her lips. Kiss it and make it her own.

So she did.

"Are you okay?" Star's eyebrows knitted and she looked at Lissa with concern. "I mean, after before." She glanced at the bed and Lissa did the same.

She couldn't believe that it was there, between her rumpled bedding and boring plain bedsheets, Star had touched her. And she had *touched Star.* It was unbelievable. It just was.

I want to do it again. It wasn't the first time she had thought that thought. And it still terrified her. There were just too many things happening for her to process it.

"Our poor cows will never make it to pasture." Star looked at her. Lissa felt it coming through her chest and bubbled out of her mouth.

They giggled and suddenly things seemed easier. Lissa didn't want things to change, for their easy friendship to disappear. And as Star made moo sounds and made her toast walk across the table, Lissa dared to hope that it wouldn't. Even though they had had sex.

"I'm okay." Lissa licked her spoon. "But are you?"

Star's eyes widened. There was no way she didn't know what Lissa meant, so Lissa waited patiently while the cogwheels in Star's brain turned.

"Want to do something?"

Lissa looked up from her plate.

Star had finished eating and was rocking on her chair. *Such a childish gesture,* Lissa thought with a grin.

"Like what?"

"Go out with me." Star rocked so far back, Lissa was worried she would fall. "I know this weekend is almost over but maybe next Friday. Or Saturday. I want to take you to *The Crying Nightingale* and dance the night away." Star's expression was unreadable.

"Is it a date?"

"I'm not going to lie." Star sounded unsure. "This isn't known ground for me. I haven't been in a relationship for a very long time, but—" She bit her lip. "—I want it to be a date. If you do too?"

How could Lissa say no?

CHAPTER SEVENTEEN

The next Friday, Lissa and Star met outside *The Crying Nightingale.* Unlike last time, the place was packed. But Star liked it. In the crowd she could pull Lissa to the dance floor and slip into anonymity. No one would bother them or stare at them in a sea of people.

The music beat through their bodies, and they had no choice but to move. Star couldn't believe everything that she was feeling; she couldn't remember a woman making her tremble this way since she was a teenager. She put her hands on Lissa's hips and held their bodies together. She couldn't bear to be further away from her. She needed Lissa close.

Her heart skipped a beat when Lissa put her arms around Star's neck and kissed her cheek before they resumed their dance.

"I feel so happy," Lissa whispered in Star's ear.

Thank God, Star thought. She wanted Lissa to like her just as much as she did. She saw desire and happiness reflected back at her, in the dim, flashing lights of the club.

The song ended and Star led Lissa to the bar, wanting a drink.

"What do you want?"

"Hmm." Lissa bit her lip again. "I've always wanted to try a sex-on-the-beach."

Star burst out laughing.

"Sure," she waved at the bartender. "A sex-on-the-beach and a beer, please."

They stood by the bar while waiting for their drinks. Star grimaced when an elbow from out of nowhere poked her in the back. Lissa smiled and shrugged, put a hand on Star's forearm and pulled her closer.

"I don't mind that it's crowded." Lissa's breath hit Star's ear and made her heart pound and her insides turn to liquid. *You need to get a grip, Star, you should have better control than this.* She couldn't remember the last time a woman had had such an effect on her.

They received their drinks and Star laughed at Lissa's delighted smile when she tried her sex-on-the-beach.

Lissa's smile disappeared and her eyes went wide.

Somebody snaked an arm around Star's middle and she was pulled into an ample chest. Star didn't care about who the hell it was, all she could see was the hurt and surprise in Lissa's eyes. *Don't worry, I still only want you.* She was ready to pounce on whoever was behind her when a mouth was placed close to her ear.

"I'm so happy I ran into you." Star recognized the voice, but couldn't remember from where. It didn't matter. It could have been anyone behind her, she would still only want to be with Lissa.

"Sorry." She turned her head and spoke loudly. "Not looking." She moved the arm away from her abdomen.

She leaned over to reach Lissa's ear.

"Want to get out of here? You've never been to my home." She finished her beer.

Lissa nodded so hard her hair bounced. Then she did her best to finish her drink in quick sips.

"Let's go." She mouthed.

Star didn't care about whoever it was behind her. A real friend wouldn't hit on her. She just grabbed Lissa's hand, left the bar, and didn't look back.

Outside it was probably cold, but Star couldn't feel it. Lissa laughed loudly.

"I can't believe you."

"What?"

"You're just so effortless to hit on. You just have to be in a bar and some lady will put her arm around you." She didn't sound insecure, but Star couldn't stop the sting of worry.

"It doesn't always happen." Star felt her cheeks heat, a rather unfamiliar feeling. She wasn't sure she liked it.

But she forgot about it when Lissa took her hand and stood on tip-toe and pressed a kiss to the side of Star's lips. She smelled like perfume and sex-on-the-beach.

Star hailed a cab.

*

Lissa was still giggling when the cab stopped and Star paid the driver. She knew it was because of the alcohol, but she didn't mind. With Star in front of her and something sweet on the tip of her tongue, she didn't think her night could get better.

She quickly changed her mind when Star unlocked her door, pulled her inside, and attacked her with her lips. Star kicked the door closed with her foot without stopping their kiss. Star's tongue was so warm inside Lissa's mouth and it made her crave things she didn't know the name of. She just knew she wanted Star and wanted her *now*.

Her eyes were closed as they kept kissing, Star guiding them through the apartment, on their way to what

Lissa assumed was the bedroom. Her apartment was considerably larger than Lissa's, and Lissa couldn't wait to inspect it further. But right now she kept her eyes firmly closed, wanting to know only Star's touch and kiss.

Star pulled her mouth away from hers, just long enough to pull her jacket off and kick her shoes to the side. Lissa did the same. Her heart was pounding, her usually buzzing mind silent. Her fingertips tingled and her lips felt swollen. She knew what she needed. What she wanted.

When Star enveloped her in an embrace again, it was as if her heart became an exclamation point. Star was so warm and smelled so great.

But they were wearing too many clothes. Lissa started to pull at Star's T-shirt, wanting it off, while she continued making content humming sounds, deep in her throat. She didn't know who she was anymore. She felt awoken, another person. Their lips met again and again. Star pulled her shirt off and Lissa's hands immediately found her breast. Star's skin was so smooth and cool under her fingertips, and she moaned when Star's nipples tightened.

"I need you, now." *Now.* She felt herself swell, almost to the point of pain, and it was only embarrassment that kept her from taking Star's hand and pressing it where she needed it the most.

Star leaned down, pulling Lissa's top up, and before she got it fully off, enveloping her nipple in her mouth. Lissa's mind filled with fireworks. Then it went blank.

"Lissa? What's happening?" Somebody patted her cheek firmly. "Honey, are you okay?"

She opened her eyes. She was lying on the bed with Star hunched over her. Star's eyes were wide and shiny, like she was close to tears. When their gazes met, Star's shoulders dropped and she blinked.

"Hey? What happened?" She pushed a hand to Lissa's shoulder. "No, don't sit up. Can I get you anything?"

Lissa chuckled. She hated that she had worried Star, but her concern was adorable.

"Please, don't worry. It happens sometimes. I probably would have noticed I was getting hungry if it wasn't for the…" She chuckled nervously. "Horniness."

"I haven't fed you dinner." Star's eyebrows knit. "I took you dancing and gave you a drink and didn't feed you dinner." Her mouth curled in annoyance.

"Don't be angry with yourself." Lissa swept her thumb over Star's mouth. "I'm a big girl, you don't need to…" She pulled her down for a quick peck. "I usually would have noticed, but the novelty of the situation made me forgot."

Star finally smiled, but the worry didn't leave her eyes.

"I'm going to order pizza, okay?"

"Okay." Lissa closed her eyes gratefully. She did feel a bit dizzy. "No cheese, please."

"One cheese-less pizza, coming up." She pressed a kiss between Lissa's eyebrows. She left Lissa alone on the bed.

Lissa turned her face and smelled the pillow under her head. *Mmm, smells like Star.* She continued to breathe slowly, trying to get the dizziness to leave her head. She couldn't believe she had actually passed out, that hadn't happened in years. She put her knees up, willing blood to flow faster to her brain. It didn't help that she was still aroused. Or that she was in Star's home.

She was actually in Star's bedroom. She opened her eyes properly, sat up. *Come on, body, don't fail me now.*

She couldn't spend her entire stay just lying in bed pathetically.

When she dared, she put her feet on the side of the bed and stood up slowly. She swayed a bit from side to side but stabilized after a little while. Then she walked over to the light switch. She needed light.

As she listened to Star talk to the pizzeria in the other room, Lissa started investigating. Four dark green walls. Wooden blinds that looked expensive. There was a shelf over the bed that had a couple of books and a jar that looked like it contained hair ties. *I wonder when Star shaved her hair off.* There was no way she needed the ties with her current hairstyle.

She turned around and looked at the other contents of the room. There was a big dresser and a closet, but Lissa wasn't going to snoop through her stuff. Even though she wanted to look. She imagined what kind of clothes Star kept in there.

Probably sex toys. She grinned. *A porn star probably owns sex toys.* She moved to the window and looked outside. *I'm glad she didn't suggest using sex toys with me. I could never...*

"Oh, good. You're up." Star had reappeared in the doorway. "How are you feeling?"

"Good." They walked closer, as if drawn by magnets. They joined hands. "Hungry."

"Well, pizza is on its way. Veggie. No cheese. Extra peppers. I hope you don't mind, I just like peppers."

"I'll pick them out." Lissa honestly didn't care, even though she hated peppers. She couldn't stop smiling.

"Which means even more peppers for me." Star grinned. "I'm really happy you feel better though. I'll remember to make sure I feed you from now on, okay?"

"You don't need to." Lissa didn't want to seem like a burden. "Seriously. I can take care of myself. You're so sweet though."

"That's me. I hide my sweetness in…" She turned red. "Damn. I was about to do a really improper joke."

"You can do that. I don't mind dirty jokes." Lissa poked a finger into Star's waist.

"Nah, when I have a lady caller, I better treat her like one."

"That happens often, then?" Lissa raised an eyebrow.

"No. First time, actually." Star's easy smile warmed her insides. "I had to be quick to find a place to store all my dirty comments and improper jokes."

"So where did you put them?" Lissa liked the joke and looked around the room.

"Next to my sex toys, naturally."

Lissa burst out laughing.

"Definitely don't want to come upon them by accident."

"Do you want to see the rest of the apartment?"

"Yeah, I'd love to."

They took a few steps toward the hallway.

"You're okay to walk around, right?" The concern in Star's voice made Lissa's heart beat a bit faster. "Not asking because I'm nice or anything, I just would hate if your heavy head dented my floor."

"If I feel dizzy, I'll tell you."

Satisfied, they walked into the hallway, but not before Star offered her an arm to hold on to. Star had turned the light on properly now and Lissa was able to see everything.

The apartment was big: two bedrooms, a spacious kitchen, and cozy living room. Much bigger than Lissa's studio.

It looked like a bachelor pad; all sleek lines, white walls, and black leather. It probably suited Star's lifestyle, and wallet, but Lissa didn't in particular like it. It was anonymous. Like Star in her movies.

"Do you spend a lot of time here?" She asked when they sat down in the kitchen by a very nice wooden table with matching chairs.

"In the kitchen?"

"No. Here. In your home." She nodded in thanks when Star put a glass of water in front of her.

"Not really." Star shrugged. "I prefer sleeping here, of course. But otherwise it's just a space that holds my stuff, you know?"

"I guess." Lissa chewed on her lip. "Your stuff."

"My stuff."

"Like your sex toys."

Star leaned back in her chair and crossed her arms over her chest. An amused light lit in her eyes.

"Yeah, what about it?"

Lissa opened her mouth when the doorbell rang.

"That must be the pizza." Star got up and went out of the kitchen. She returned within a few minutes carrying a pizza box. She put it between them on the table and opened it.

Lissa didn't even say thanks, she was so hungry that she just grabbed a slice. She didn't care that Star laughed at her eagerness.

She ate several slices in silence, then wiped her mouth with the back of her sleeve, not caring how she seemed. Star had also eaten in the meantime.

"So." Lissa said, wondering if she would dare. "Sex toys."

"What about them?"

"Tell me about it." Lissa leaned forward. "All of it. You have… you have sex with people for a living. I don't understand it. I want to understand it."

"What is it about it that you don't understand?"

"How you can have sex with so many different people. I like sex." Star gave her a look. "I mean, I love sex with you. Eh, I mean." She cleared her throat. Star laughed.

"Are you asking me if sex is less special to me because I do it for living?" Star looked completely calm.

"Kind of. Maybe." Lissa wanted to know Star's answer even if that wasn't the question she had wanted to ask from the beginning. She was worried her questions were going to upset Star though.

"Maybe sex isn't a holy experience for me. That doesn't mean it isn't special." Star sighed and looked like she was thinking. "I love sex. I love sex with women. I love finding out what makes them tick. I also like acting. I like being silly. I like orgasms. I have a pretty strong exhibition kink which makes having sex on a screen that much sweeter. I love that people appreciate it in a special type of way. And sometimes—" she nudged Lissa's toe under the table with her own. "—sometimes I get the delicious experience of meeting someone who clearly is recognizing me from somewhere but doesn't want to admit from where."

"Does that happen often?"

"Nope." Star chuckled. "And I only really take notice when the person in question has that look in her face of a woman who really isn't much more than an innocent little girl."

Lissa pouted. "I'm not an innocent little girl."

There were loads of things that Star could have answered to this. Lissa could imagine all the teasing remarks. '*Not once I'm through with you, you won't be, no.*' '*It's cute that you think so.*' But she didn't say anything. She was waiting for Lissa's reply, but Lissa didn't know what to say.

"So?" Star said eventually. "Do you judge what I do? Do you wish I did something else?"

"Both yes and no." Lissa didn't want to lie. "Don't get me wrong, you're gorgeous. Everything about you is gorgeous. Your job makes you even hotter." She chewed on her lip.

"You're worried what people would think?" The words must have hurt Star, but she still said them. *She wants to help me figure this out.*

"It's stupid. I mean, I doubt my mother would approve, but she's not even here anymore." Sadness welled up inside her. "There is no one left to disapprove."

"*I* have a question for *you*."

"Yeah?" Lissa looked up.

"How do you suppose this relationship will work?" Star's features had smoothed out while they were talking. They had smoothed out so much that they conveyed no emotions. "If I tell you I'm working in a few days, how does that make you feel?" She kept looking at Lissa, but she wasn't there anymore. "How about when I go partying for several days and don't call?"

Is she so scared of my answer that she emotionally checked out?

Lissa didn't like it. It reminded her of how much she didn't know about Star. She didn't know her past. She didn't know about past relationships. She didn't know how Star reacted to stuff.

"I honestly don't know." Lissa wanted to give Star an answer, but she didn't know how she felt. Things were happening too fast. "I don't think I'm jealous of your job. I *like* watching you." She felt herself blush. "I don't think I'd like if you go cruising, but I'm a busy person too. I need my downtime just like you. If partying makes you happy, I wouldn't think of standing in your way. I wouldn't want to introduce you to people as 'my girlfriend the porn star,' but that's how I feel right now. Who knows how I will feel in ten weeks' time." She cringed at the word *girlfriend,* but she was only using it to convey what she wanted.

"Ten weeks' time?" Star's lips curled into grin.

"Well… five weeks seemed kind of short, but I didn't dare to suggest twenty." She dared to smile when Star chuckled at her.

"You are so adorable." Star stood up, leaned across the table, and pressed a kiss to Lissa's nose. "So we date for ten weeks then follow up on our mutual experience?"

Lissa's heart started beating hard. She almost didn't dare to guess what Star was really saying.

"That seems wise." She nodded. "Maybe we could have bi-weekly follow-ups. To make sure that we're going where we want to go."

"Should we write an action plan?"

Lissa nodded. She didn't care that Star was messing with her.

"I'll prepare a binder for our next meeting so we can document everything."

"Documenting now?" Star leaned back. "Maybe we should talk about this, I'm really not ready for binders and documenting."

"Yeah, me neither." Lissa giggled. She looked down on the empty pizza box. She felt very content. And excited. Her life had been nothing but exciting since meeting Star.

"Can I ask you something else?" Star's question made her look up again.

"Anything."

"Why were you a virgin? Not that there's anything wrong with it. I'm just curious. It's not very common. I know I asked before, but back then you just said you weren't interested. Honestly, is it really just that?"

Lissa felt the blood run from her face and she cleared her throat, looking for words.

"There isn't really a real reason." *What can I say?* "It just didn't happen. I was busy with work, busy with university. Since I didn't really drink, I never had the experience of a drunken one-night-stand. Plus the gay thing, you know? I don't really move much in lesbian circles. My friends aren't gay, and I don't meet a lot of other gay women. One day I just turned twenty-three, figured there was something wrong with me and gave up."

"There was never anything wrong with you," Star said slowly.

"I know." Lissa smiled. "But knowing and feeling are two different things."

Their hands met across the table.

"What about you?"

"What about me?"

Lissa ran her thumb over Star's knuckles.

"You like me. Why did you only want to be friends?"

Star's phone rang, lying at the end of the table.

"Excuse me." Star palmed it, pressed a button, and placed the phone against her ear.

Lissa looked on as Star's face visibly paled and her lower lip trembled.

"Thank you." She didn't sound like herself. She ended the call and put her phone on the table. She didn't look at Lissa.

"What happened?"

"My mom died. Her heart gave out." The words were quick. Void of emotion. She wouldn't meet Lissa's gaze.

"Oh my God, Star." Lissa had to swallow back immediate tears. She hated that parents had to die. "I'm so, so sorry. Are you okay?"

"I'm okay." Star sighed. "Listen, I think it's time to call it a night."

"No, Star. You can't be alone right now."

Star looked up at her. Her eyes were darker now, and even though her lower lip still trembled, she looked more angry than sad.

"No."

Abruptly, Star got up and walked towards the door. She stood in the kitchen doorway on the side as if expecting Lissa to leave.

Lissa kicked her chair back and got up. She walked toward the hallway, her eyes never leaving Star's face.

"I want to be with you." She sounded like a needy child and hated it. "Please."

Star put a hand on her lower back and gently pushed her towards the door.

They stopped by her front door.

"I need to deal with this by myself." Star handed her her jacket. "Okay?" She leaned forward and kissed her forehead. Her lips were cold. So different from their earlier fire. "I'll call you tomorrow."

"Okay." Lissa put on her jacket and her shoes. *I don't want to leave her.*

Who knew what Star was really feeling. Lissa was again reminded that she didn't actually know Star. They had only known each other for a couple of weeks. Their usually amazing connection didn't matter. They didn't know each other.

Star squeezed Lissa's hand one more time while she opened her door and motioned for Lissa to walk through it.

"Thanks." Her smile was a grimace and her eyes were filled with pain. "Bye."

The door was slammed in Lissa's face.

CHAPTER EIGHTEEN

I wonder how Star is doing. Lissa groaned at her thoughts. It had been three days and she couldn't get her out of her head. *I wish she had called.* Lissa had both called and sent messages, but Star hadn't replied. After three days of moping at home, Lissa forced herself out of her house. She'd gone to town, looking at color schemes for the next party. It wasn't for another two weeks, but she needed to get out of the house. She was going crazy just waiting around at home.

She picked up a green candle stick, playing with the idea of a silver-forest theme when a store clerk spoke behind her.

"You need some help?"

Lissa turned around to say no but was met by the sight of Malena. At first she couldn't place her and just stared.

"Malena." Malena pointed at herself. "I'm Star's friend. We met a few weeks ago?"

"Yes! Of course I remember you." *How could I forget?* "Hi!"

"Hey!" Malena's smile was infectious. "How are you?"

Have you heard from Star? "I'm fine. And you?"

"Blech. Working." Malena laughed. "Almost forty and still don't know what I want to do when I grow up."

A man who walked by wearing a manager's vest coughed at her, but Malena just rolled her eyes.

"Okay, after that line I probably should at least pretend to work for a bit. But I have lunch in thirty minutes." She looked at Lissa with a pointed look in her face.

"Oh." Lissa's heart rushed. "Want to have lunch?"

"Meet me at the *Subway* across the street, yeah?" Malena winked and then hurried away.

Lissa watched her leave. *What had just happened?* She looked at the candle stick still in her hand. She put it back. It wasn't like she was actually getting anything anyway.

*

"Sorry I'm late!" Malena pulled her in for a quick hug. Lissa didn't know what to do with her hands as she was enveloped in a cloud of perfume with soft breasts pressed against her throat.

"That's fine," Lissa coughed out. "I was looking at shoes until just a few minutes ago."

"Good, good." They entered the building. "I hope you don't mind eating here. Sometimes I just feel like it, you know?"

"It's no problem," Lissa said while looking at the menu. Eventually she settled for a Veggie Delite.

They got their sandwiches. Malena also grabbed a packet of chips and then sat down by a table in a corner.

"I'm so happy that I ran into you." Malena started with the chips first.

"Really?" Lissa's eyes went wide. "But why?"

"Because you," Malena pointed a chip in her direction. "You're the little minx who has ensnared my friend."

137

"Ensnared?" *Minx?* Lissa blinked. "What?"

Malena nodded. There were lines of worry around her eyes.

"Have you heard from her?" Lissa couldn't wait to ask.

"No. Why?" She crumbled the now empty chip packet. "You're the first one she's ever talked to me about. That way." She leaned forward, chin in hands. "It's made me terribly curious."

Lissa blinked again, unsure of what to say. Unsure what to feel.

"I'm honored, I guess." She made a painful grimace. "I don't know what to reply to that to be honest." She drew in a shaky breath. "Have you really not heard from her?"

"Why?" Malena sounded worried now. "Has something happened?"

Lissa swallowed. The bites of the sandwich were just growing in her mouth.

"Her mom died."

"Poor Star." Malena sighed deeply. "She must be so confused." Their eyes met. "I don't mean to be cold, but her mom has given her enough grief." She reached out and grabbed Lissa's hand. "If she was in the right mind to call you, she would have."

Lissa shook her head. "It's just killing me that I can't help her. Can't support her. Can't comfort her."

"Well, that's how Star is." Malena dug into her sandwich once again. "Sorry," she said with her mouthful. "I just have to go back to work eventually. Need to eat up before that."

"Don't worry," Lissa said. "Feel free."

"It's how she's always been," Malena said when she'd finished chewing. "She gets into these moods where she just ignores everyone. Once I didn't hear from her from two months, even though I kept calling her."

Lissa's eyes went wide.

"But why? Two months?" *If I don't hear from her for that long, I don't know what I'm going to do.*

"Yes. But don't worry, that doesn't mean it's going to happen to you." Malena finished the last of her sandwich in two quick bites. "If you don't hear from her within the next couple of days we'll storm her apartment, okay?"

"Fine." But she didn't feel fine. "You must have known her for a long time, I guess?"

Malena nodded.

"We have been friends since first grade. Star, Deirdre, and I. Three Musketeers." She looked at her watch. "Damn, I really need to go. But hey, we should hang out sometime," she said in a lighter tone. "I know everything is crazy now, but it won't always be. I want to be friends with you. If that's okay."

"It's okay." Lissa tried to smile— it felt better than she thought it would. "More than okay."

*

After Malena left Star's cute, little friend, she hurried off back to work. Her manager would be pissed, but he was always pissed with her. She hoped that he wouldn't fire her. Her resume didn't look too good anymore.

She was right by the entrance to the store when she stopped for a second. Took out her phone and quickly typed a message.

I heard about your mom. I'm so sorry, sweetheart. Please call Lissa, okay? She's worried about you.

Kathy L. Salt

I'm here if you need to talk.
Love you,
M

CHAPTER NINETEEN

Star tried to suppress a yawn. She knew that she had to uphold some semblance of grief to the funeral director and Natasha, who had invited herself. The truth was that she was just feeling numb, surreal. She wanted to be anywhere other than where she was. She calculated the time it would take her to get to her car and drive to Lissa's. She had said she would call and she still hadn't, she hadn't been able to make herself do it. It had been three days. *I suck, she must think I'm—*

"Miss Ciel?"

"Huh?"

The funeral director was looking at her.

"Yes. Sorry." She stopped a yawn. *Stop being ridiculous, Star. Pay attention. Act like an adult for once in your life.*

"You've decided on no cremation and a pine casket. So it's really just a matter of planning the memorial." He sighed.

"I think your mother would have preferred to have a eulogist. And somebody should sing, maybe *Angel*," Natasha said.

Well, who asked you, Star thought. She kicked back on her chair, feeling like a child again. She just wanted to get out of there. She would have given anything to be back in Lissa's apartment, playing that ridiculously wonderful cow game. She would have given anything to be back in Lissa's bed, just sleeping in each other's arms.

"Well then, I think we're done here." The funeral director closed his file and handed Star a bundle of papers. "Deepest condolences, Miss Ciel, but I hope you'll be happy with our services."

"Thank you." Star shook his hand. His hand was course against her skin. *Has he ever used hand cream in his life?* It was bothering her, and she felt like ripping her hand from his. *Get a grip, Star, you're losing it.*

She paid and then she was finally able to leave.

She walked out of the building with Natasha. Nothing felt real.

"Do you want to go for a coffee?"

Star stared at the other woman.

"No." She shook her head. "I don't want to go for a coffee. I want to rob a liquor store, take my loot home, and have a very, very good night." At that moment she meant every word.

"Star," Natasha hissed. "How can you say that?"

Star bared her teeth. "I want to see how much body-water percentage I can turn to ethanol."

The nurse pursed her lips, looking like she wanted to say something else.

"I guess I'll see you at the funeral then."

"You guess right." Star turned around and started walking. She didn't care to look back, slamming her feet into the concrete with each step. She didn't even know why she was so angry.

She walked by the river, wondering what to do next. She didn't want to go home alone and she didn't want company either. And in spite of what she had said to

Natasha, she really didn't want to inhale alcohol until she forgot everything.

She stopped and turned toward the water, leaned her arms on the rails. *I just want to be normal.* She wanted a normal life. With a normal mom. A normal, alive mom.

And a normal job. She growled toward a man who leered at her. She was too fed up with all this. She sighed and pulled the collar of her jacket higher around her neck. She was mainly doing it to hide as much as possible, but she was also increasingly cold. Summer was truly over.

Her phone beeped and she took it out, finding a text from Malena. She stared at it in disbelief. *At least I have good friends.* That she did. She had friends who stayed with her even when she ignored them. *But Lissa might not.* Lissa didn't know her yet, Star couldn't know that she would wait around, especially when Star didn't keep her promise to call.

"I'm an idiot," Star said out loud. Then she called Lissa.

"Star!" Lissa's voice felt like a million hugs and Christmas and an orgasm, all rolled into one. "Hello." Star should have called her days ago, she should have known that talking to Lissa would have made her feel better, not worse.

"Hi." Star closed her eyes. "Sorry that I haven't called before this."

"Don't be ridiculous." Lissa clicked her tongue. "You've been busy."

"And sad." Star had to say it.

"Do you want to meet? I… it would be nice to give you a hug." She sounded so unsure, it broke Star's heart.

"Not right now." She didn't like rejecting Lissa, but she needed to be alone for a few more days. "The funeral is on Friday. I'll call you after, okay?"

"Want me to come to the funeral?"

"No." Star loved her for offering. "I'll call you after, okay?"

"I'm working on Friday, but we can meet up early on Saturday? I work that night though." Lissa sounded like she was holding her breath.

"Sure." Star felt that her mouth was smiling, even if she didn't properly feel it inside. She grabbed the rails with the hand not holding her phone and leaned backwards. "Hey, Lissa?"

"Yes?"

"I'm so sorry for throwing you out the other day. I just panicked and didn't know what to do."

Lissa didn't answer and Star waited.

"I won't lie," she said after a while. "It made me sad, but not as sad as I got when you said you'd call and then didn't for several days. I think I'd have preferred if you just told me that you'd call when you were ready."

"I'll do that next time." Star leaned against the rail. "Sometimes I just need to be alone. I've ignored people for months before."

"I know." Lissa sounded tired. "Malena told me."

Malena?

"I don't want to do that to you. Now that I called you, I realized how stupid I had been." Star closed her eyes. "The moment I heard your voice I felt a hundred times better."

"Oh, Star." Lissa's voice was soft.

"Well." Star cleared her throat. "I'll see you Saturday then."

"Star?"

"Yes."

"Why can't we see each other now?"

"I'm not ready to see anyone yet." Star wanted to continue with what she'd been doing for the past couple of days; drinking herself to sleep. But she didn't want to tell Lissa that.

"Fine." Lissa sighed. "I'll see you Saturday then."

Star wanted to say something else, but she couldn't, so she just turned off the call and swallowed back tears.

CHAPTER TWENTY

Lissa stared at her phone. It had probably been over five minutes since Star had rung, but she couldn't put her phone down. She wanted Star to call again. Part of the wish was selfish. She wanted to hear Star's voice. She wanted to ask her if she was okay. She wanted to hear Star say that she couldn't wait to see her.

The other part of the wish was concern. Since Star had received the call that her mother had died, she had turned into another person, and she had shut Lissa out. That had stung. But it also meant that Lissa couldn't tell if Star was okay. She couldn't hold her, comfort her. Help her. It felt like Star had given her the world and Lissa had nothing to give back.

She jumped when the phone started buzzing in her hand. The number was unknown which probably meant potential client.

"Hello, *Yolanda's Events and Cake Center*. Lissa speaking, how may I help?"

As she listened to the woman she felt a headache coming. This was so not what she wanted to do with her life. She took the woman's details and ended the call as soon as she could. She quickly dialed Yolanda's number.

"Hi, it's Lissa." She waited for Yolanda to get through her usual pleasantries. She could almost hear her long nails clicking against the phone. "We had a woman just call in. She wants us to set up a birthday party for..." Her mouth almost didn't want to say the words. "...for her dog Vincent. Preferably within the next two weeks. The date doesn't need to be perfect, as it's not the actual date of his birth, but rather the day they adopted him." *My job is stupid. Worthless.* She gritted her teeth. She couldn't do this anymore.

"Okay," Yolanda said. "Well, we'll look in the calendar; that female couple, Ingrid and Helen, personally asked for you to plan their engagement party, and we have Olivia Johansson's sweet sixteen."

Lissa counted in her head. With all those parties she would be very busy for the next three weeks. Maybe four. Maybe five. Sure the money would be rolling in, but with all that work she wouldn't have time to see Star. Maybe that thought was idiotic. But she also wouldn't have time for herself. And it was one thing to be busy with a job that she actually liked or knew was worthwhile. It was different to be bored out of her mind at some dumb-ass—

"Yolanda?" She cut her off. "I can't do this anymore."

Yolanda turned silent.

"What?"

"I'm sorry. I'm resigning. I want to do something else."

Yolanda sighed.

"Well, I get that, sweetheart, but you can't just leave me like this all of a sudden. Why don't you keep your job while looking for what you want to do?"

"Sorry." Lissa knew that she was letting her down, but she had to follow her heart. "I'll take the engagement party next week, but why don't you ask Mollie to take the others? I know Peter is free this week too."

"Don't decide just yet!" Yolanda sounded a bit desperate now. "Let's meet this afternoon."

Lissa sighed and closed her eyes. She couldn't deal with this right now.

"Fine," she said eventually. "We can talk, but trust me, it won't change anything."

She didn't want to just leave Yolanda out of nowhere, but she knew that she had other girls, plus her employment was basically a freelance position. Yolanda couldn't legally force her to keep working. She didn't even need to leave a two-weeks notice. She couldn't leave Yolanda with three open jobs, but she could leave her with two.

They set up the appointment and hung up. Lissa put her phone on the table and got up. She didn't want to sit down anymore. She was going to go out for a run.

CHAPTER TWENTY-ONE

It was quarter-past-three on Saturday afternoon when Star met Lissa by the beach. Lissa had expected, and hoped, that once the funeral was over Star would be relieved. But there was a raw edge to her voice and there was tension in her shoulders that made Lissa want to hug her.

Star was still wearing her funeral clothes, a black fitted suit with rolled up sleeves. It was strange to see her in such formal clothing.

"Hi." Lissa wanted to hug her but kept her distance. She didn't know if her touch would be welcome.

"Hi." Star opened her arms and Lissa stepped into them, gratefully.

They hugged for a few silent minutes, let go, and walked along the water line side by side.

"Did the funeral go well?" The question sounded lame in her own ears too.

"She's in the ground." Star sighed. "It's sad that her sister couldn't make it."

"Were there a lot of people there?" Lissa couldn't believe she was sounding so normal when all she wanted to do was grab Star's shoulder and shake her. Ask her how she was, where they stood. Why she had to keep everyone at an arm's length.

Star looked up at the sky and laughed mirthlessly.

"It was me and the pastor."

"I could have gone and—"

"No." Star didn't let her finish. "I didn't want you there."

She left Lissa on the path and walked toward the water, picked up something in the sand—a seashell or a small rock—and threw it toward the gentle waves.

What should I do? Lissa wanted to comfort her somehow. Say the right words. Offer the right things. She walked up next to Star. She also wanted to punch her a little bit.

"Maybe I should have gone there anyway. Even if you didn't want me there."

Star sighed but didn't answer. She picked up another rock and threw it in the water.

"I loved her a lot, you know."

"I don't doubt that. She was your mother."

"I..." Her voice broke momentarily, but then she started talking. "When I was still a child she used to have these parties. She would be surrounded by so many people who loved her. And she would laugh and dance and sing. And she would wear these colorful dresses that made her hair shine as she moved to the music." She sighed and Lissa pretended not to see the tears running down her cheeks. "She was so beautiful. So alive. I loved her." More tears came. "I'd like to think that she loved me too."

Of course she did. In Lissa's mind there was no question about it, but it was as if her lips were sealed with glue. She couldn't say anything. Even when Star burst out in tears.

But she could comfort her physically. She wrapped her arms around Star's shoulders and held her close. Her heart ached when Star put her arms around her waist and pushed her face into her neck. Her whole body was shaking with sobs, and Lissa could do nothing but just hold her close.

They stood like that for several minutes, the wind pulling at Lissa's hair and their clothes. It was a bit chilly, but not too much. Especially not when you were deep in an embrace.

Eventually, Star pulled back a bit and looked down at Lissa. Her lips were a bit swollen from all the crying which made them look all that more kissable. *Shut up, brain,* Lissa thought. Star was the one who initiated a kiss though.

Their lips met in a slow kiss that tasted of either sea or tears. It didn't matter, it warmed Lissa from the tips of her toes to her heart and head. It wasn't an arousing kiss. It just sealed their feelings and was a way for Lissa to speak. *I'm here for you. If you want me I'm yours. You don't have to be alone anymore.* Lissa knew that these things were too early to say. That didn't mean that she wasn't allowed to feel them.

"Thank you for meeting me," Star said when their kiss ended naturally. "And thank you for this."

"That's okay." Lissa pressed a kiss to her cheek. "I wasn't working today anyway." *What kind of stupid lame ass answer was that?*

Her embarrassment must have shown because Star just chuckled.

"Sorry for getting you all wet. I didn't mean for that to happen." She wiped Lissa's neck with the sleeve of her jacket. "I guess I'm more upset than I thought I was." She turned toward the sea again but kept Lissa close with an arm around her shoulders. "Oh, Lissa. Her funeral was so dreary. All her friends are either gone, dead, or in a home somewhere. There was nothing of that smiling woman from my childhood. She would have hated it."

"I'm sorry," Lissa whispered. "Maybe we can do something? Have a party in her honor or something."

"No." Star sighed. "But thanks for offering. It's time to look to the future."

"Yeah." It was Lissa's turn to sigh. She still couldn't believe she had quit her job. What else was she supposed to do now?

"You're not working today?"

Lissa shook her head.

"I thought you were booked up almost every weekend until—"

"I was." Lissa interrupted her. "I'm not anymore. I…" She couldn't suppress a nervous giggle. "I quit my job."

"What?" Star turned her around with hands to her shoulders. "You quit your job? When did that happen?"

Lissa felt her face break out in a grin. It was scary, but she really was very pleased.

"Last week. I just felt it was time."

"Wow!" Star smiled. "You look so happy that I feel like congratulations are in order."

"Thanks." Lissa laughed.

"So what are you going to do now?"

"I have no idea." Lissa continued laughing. "But I'll figure it out. I always do."

"I wish you luck then." Star looked thoughtful.

"What?" Lissa searched her gaze. "What is it?"

"Oh, nothing. Just a bit jealous of your bravery. Maybe I should quit too."

"So, do." Lissa smiled teasingly. "Let me tell you, there is nothing more invigorating."

"You're crazy." Star rustled her hair.

The movement caused goose bumps to travel down her spine and she involuntarily shivered.

"Are you cold?"

"A little." Lissa hugged herself. "But it's okay if you want to stay."

"I don't." Star grabbed her hand. "Let's go and grab a pizza. I'm hungry."

CHAPTER TWENTY-TWO

Star was happy that Lissa didn't question when she ordered their cheese-less pizza with eggplant and sun-dried tomatoes to go. She didn't want to engage in mindless conversation in the middle of the pizzeria. All she wanted was to go home with her pizza and her girl and put on a movie. Turn her brain off for a bit. She hoped that Lissa wouldn't mind too much.

I wonder what she's thinking. Lissa wasn't looking at her, but at her phone. Star had both ordered and paid and now she was unsure what to do with the ten to twenty minutes they had to wait.

"Mind if we eat at home?"

"Of course not."

"I was thinking we could watch a movie. Action maybe. Something that we can just look at and not think." She looked pleadingly at Lissa.

Lissa just nodded.

"Whatever you want is fine." She grabbed Star's hand and gave it a comforting squeeze.

Whatever I want. What did Star want? She didn't know anymore. Maybe she had never known.

They got their pizza and walked back to Star's place. Neither of them talked. Lissa had a distant look in her face and Star felt equally lost for words. What could you say after a day like theirs?

When they arrived at her door she almost apologized, saying she needed to call to check on Hawke. She realized with a sigh that she would never have to do that again. Hawke didn't need her anymore. She was free. But also lonely in a way that she had actually never been before. Her mother, no matter how useless, had always existed in the background.

She let them both into her apartment.

"Just go into the living room. I'll bring plates and stuff. What do you want to drink? I have beer."

"Just water, please." Lissa took the pizza with her and disappeared down the hall.

Star took a swift breath of relief. It was nicer to be alone. With Lissa it felt like she had to keep it together. Couldn't scream. Couldn't cry. But she didn't want to do those things. What she needed was some form of blackout. Some means to close her brain off. A pizza and a movie would have to do. Because the other thing she needed, she really couldn't ask of Lissa.

She sighed and went back into the living room.

Lissa looked up as she came in and suddenly all of Star's wishes and needs were met. Not by the beer in her hand. Not by the pizza, even though food was welcome. And even though she did want to watch the movie, what she needed was right in front of her, in the shape of Lissa.

"Hi." Star sat down in front of her and kissed her on the lips. "Thank you for being here."

"You're welcome." Lissa's smile was home. "I'm not exactly sacrificing anything though."

Star dimmed the light and put the movie on. Then they dug into the pizza. Star had to give it to Lissa, cheese-less pizza was much better than she could have ever thought. There was no talk of separation, they just ate, finished the movie, and then went to the bathroom.

"You can borrow my toothbrush." Star kissed her cheek and went to bed. She just knew that Lissa would follow her into the bedroom once she was done.

She took off her clothes and crawled under the covers completely naked.

*

Lissa folded her clothes and put them on top of a chair in the bathroom, then she slipped into the bedroom naked. It was exhilarating to walk around in Star's apartment buck naked, cold air touching her everywhere.

She stood by the doorway, looking at the small figure on the bed. She knew that Star was hurting and she wished she could do something help. She crawled under the covers and folded herself around Star's curled-up form. She put her arm around Star's middle and put her cheek against Star's shoulder. Star was trembling slightly, but Lissa didn't know if it was because she was crying or she was cold. She stroked her hand up and down. Star groaned.

"You okay?" She whispered.

Muscles tensed under her dancing fingers.

"Just feeling a bit tense." Star placed her hand on top of Lissa's. "Your touch is…" She sighed deeply.

She needs me. Lissa's heart hurt. She palmed the skin under her fingers and put her hand lower. When her fingers reached smooth, shaved skin Star moaned and stopped her hand.

"Please stop it. I'm too tired to do anything." Her breath was ragged.

"You don't have to." Lissa pressed a kiss to behind Star's ear. "Just relax. I'll take care of you."

Lissa had seen enough of Star's videos to know that she usually was the most active partner in the bedroom. Maybe it was good for her to be passive for once.

"But—"

"Shh..." Lissa put her other hand under Star's face and placed her hand over Star's mouth.

She trusted that it wouldn't scare her. Maybe she would even like it. *I don't think I would like anyone holding their hand over....* She shivered inwardly. *Okay, maybe I would like it.* She filed it away to think about later. Now she needed to focus on Star.

Star's reaction was immediate. Her body became stiff as a board and she arched, pushing her face into Lissa's hand. She produced a loud groan.

I guessed right... A wave of triumph flew through Lissa. She held Star close and put her other hand lower, her fingers gliding through smooth skin. She found her clit and pressed. Stroking it up and down.

Star's whole being pounded, and even though her movements were sloppy, she managed to rock her hips against Lissa's hand. The flesh under Lissa's fingertips throbbed.

"Want me to go inside?"

"Mmmhmm."

Lissa didn't remove her hand over Star's mouth but pressed down harder as the fingers on her other hand found their way inside. She couldn't really process what she was doing or how she knew what to do. But somehow she knew exactly what Star needed.

She started a thrusting motion with her hand while holding on tight, not letting Star move around as much as she wanted. The lack of mobility seemed to have the desired effect. Star's whole body trembled. and she was producing sounds deep in her throat. It was warm under the covers, and they both started to sweat as Lissa's hips started rocking against Star's ass, as if they had a life on their own.

"Lissa." Star's voice was muffled, but it was clear whose name it was that she said. "I want to come."

Lissa wanted to make her come.

"Just…" Lissa's voice was strangely dark. She tried to thrust harder with her hand, but her own muscles were burning and she had started to shake. *Please, please, please, please.*

"Mmmmhhhmm." Star came with a strangled moan, going limp in Lissa's arms.

Lissa took her hand away from Star's mouth but didn't want to leave the warm, wet haven that her other fingers had found.

"You've ruined me," Star hissed. "Broken my heart. Destroyed me."

Lissa didn't know what to answer, so she just held her close until Star's breathing evened and every limb relaxed.

"I love you." Lissa whispered into the night.

CHAPTER TWENTY-THREE

Vanille laughed. A bubbly, wild laughter that used to make Star tingle inside. Vanille was an old favorite of Star's, they had always had amazing chemistry. Vanille was just Star's type too; fair, tall, busty. Star had especially enjoyed the way she was so ticklish.

They kissed. Star closed her eyes and tried to ignore the pounding headache she was developing just beneath her temples. She deepened the kiss and pushed Vanille on her back. The goal was to eventually ride Vanille's face, but they were still a long way from there.

Vanille moaned and rubbed herself against Star's naked leg. Star's body responded as it should. She felt herself grow hot and heavy. But her mind was somewhere else.

"Tara," Vanille whimpered as she grabbed Star's butt. She held her close.

"Take your shirt off." Star pulled away from Vanille's grip and sat up. Then she helped Vanille with her shirt and also took off her own. They were both naked now, and Vanille's sultry moan managed to make Star even wetter.

Vanille put her hands in Star's hair and Star kissed her way to Vanille's ample bosom. She placed one hand on Vanille's left breast, pinching the nipple between her thumb and forefinger. She sucked Vanille's other nipple into her mouth.

Kathy L. Salt

I miss Lissa. The stray thought entered her head, not fully welcome.

Lissa's smile. Lissa's kisses. Lissa's touch.

Vanille moaned again.

"I want to taste you."

"Mmm." Star willed Lissa to leave her head, but it wasn't so easy.

She sat up with one leg on each side of Vanille's abdomen. She rubbed herself on Vanille's stomach while kneading her chest.

"You want to taste me, huh?" She forced her voice to be low. Her Tara-voice. When all she wanted to be was Star.

"Please." Vanille put her open palms on Star's ass and pushed, moving her forward. "Oh God, you're so wet."

Star cringed inwardly.

"You want this?" She opened herself with one hand and swayed teasingly toward Vanille's face. *God, who wrote this dialogue?*

"Yes, please!" Vanille managed one final shove and put her tongue on Star's heated flesh.

Star groaned at the contact.

"Suck me."

"Oh, yes! Yes, yes, yes." Star rode Vanille's face hard, eventually giving up on fighting it. She was going to come, and she would come with Lissa's face on the back of her eyelids. Nothing mattered anymore. Star finally knew what she had to do.

*

Stargazing

As soon as the filming was done, she said bye to Vanille and the director and more or less ran from the set. She hailed a cab and went home.

She unlocked her door and went inside, threw her jacket on the floor, not caring where it landed. She went straight into her bedroom and took off her jeans and T-shirt. She was wearing nothing underneath. *Classy, Star.* She laughed at herself.

She went into the bathroom and turned the shower on. She needed to get clean.

When she got out of the shower, she put the towel on the bed and laid down on it, wanting to let her skin dry on its own. She grabbed her phone and checked her Twitter while she dried. It was her favorite way to relax after a shower, one she didn't allow herself often.

When her hair was almost dry, she texted Lissa.

There's something I'd like to talk to you about.
Are you home?

The answer came within a few minutes.

I'm at the supermarket right now, but I'll be home in twenty.
Feel free to come around whenever you want.

Star looked at her phone and smiled. She had never felt more clear of mind.

*

An hour later, Star found herself outside Lissa's door with a pounding heart and a huge smile on her face. She rang the doorbell, fighting down the nervous butterflies fluttering in the pit of her stomach.

Lissa opened the door and invited her in. They kissed as a greeting.

"What's wrong with you?" Lissa giggled as she looked at her. "You look like you've seen a ghost, but a flowery ghost with a smiling face."

"What?" Star felt like laughing as well. She made sure that the door was closed and then she turned back to Lissa. "Go abroad with me."

"What?" Lissa's mouth fell open. "Did you hit your head or something?"

"No. But I don't want to do this anymore." Star grabbed her hand. "I quit my job. You quit your job. Let's go away. To somewhere warm. Like Thailand. India. Dubai. Greece. Anywhere."

"We don't even know each other." Lissa's face her turned a cute shade of pink lemonade, but there was a small smile playing on her lips. *She thinks I'm joking.*

Star wasn't joking.

"So let's get to know each other in Dubai. Or Copenhagen. Or Thailand. Just please, let's get out of here."

Lissa put her hand on Star's cheek.

"It's sweet that you would think of me." She kissed her gently. "But we can't go. Even if we don't have jobs. Even if… you just lost your mother. We can't just *leave*. No buts." She put a hand on Star's lips to silence her. "Come to the table."

Lissa led her to her little table and put Star on one of the chairs. Instead of sitting down on the other chair, she sat down on Star's lap and put her arms around Star's neck.

Star put her hand on Lissa's waist.

"Crazy, wonderful, Star," Lissa whispered and kissed her. "We can't go. I love the idea, but it's too crazy for me, okay?" Her eyes were shiny, staring into Star's soul. She looked worried.

"I think you're wrong." Star hid her face in the crook of Lissa's neck, feeling a bit embarrassed. "But I guess it was a bit crazy." She pressed her lips to Lissa's neck.

"It was a good crazy!" Lissa hugged her close. "If we had known each other for longer, maybe I'd have said…"

Her phone rang.

"Oh, sorry." Lissa jumped off Star's lap. She picked up her phone. "I got to take this." She answered.

While Lissa talked on the phone, Star got up and got herself a glass of water.

"There, sorry about that." Lissa put her phone on the table.

"That's okay. You look happy."

Lissa shone like a beacon. She grabbed Star's hand.

"I got a job!"

"Oh, yay!" Star's face broke out in a smile. "That's great news! And you look so happy. What job is it?"

"It's a position as an educational administrator at Bingley Middle School."

"Educational administrator." Star couldn't help but chuckle. Lissa looked so happy, she couldn't help but be happy with her, even though she didn't understand why an administrator position was anything to celebrate.

"I know it's silly."

Star didn't think she'd ever seen a smile so wide.

"But I can't wait."

"I'm happy for you." Star pulled her in for a hug. "When do you start?"

"Not until the first of November, when their current one goes on maternity leave. It's good that I have a lot saved up." November was still three months away. Still plenty of time for a trip, but Star didn't bring it up again.

"What are you going to do?" Lissa ran her hand down Star's arm, causing goose bumps to form.

"I have no idea." Star ran her fingers through her hair. But she didn't feel worried, she felt free. "Maybe I'll study something."

"That sounds like a good idea." Lissa swayed their joined hands. "So you're free for the rest of the day?" She winked.

"Right." Star put her hand around Lissa's waist. "What do you have in mind?"

Lissa giggled, stood on tiptoe and whispered into Star's ear.

"Want to finish our crazy cow game?"

CHAPTER TWENTY-FOUR

It was the next weekend, and Lissa was lying on her bed, reading a magazine. Dea was lying on the bed too, resting her head on Lissa's lap. On the sofa sat Grayson, playing on a handheld video gaming device.

Lissa rested one hand in her sister's hair. It felt like the past. The past when they were still in high school and would spend the afternoon just being in each other's company. She was happy that Dea and Grayson had decided to spend the weekend with her in the city. It also gave them a chance to go out all together. Lissa had planned it all out. Star was going out with a group of friends too, and Lissa was too shy to go by herself.

"So can I really go to this thing?" Grayson said. He hadn't taken his gaze from the video game and his fingers were constantly pressing buttons.

Dea and Lissa shared a look.

"Why?" Dea eventually asked.

"Is it a woman's bar we're going to?"

"Grayson," Dea sat up. "Just turn the game off when you're talking with me."

He clicked on a button, the sound went away, and he looked up.

"Are you sure it's fine if I go?" He threw a look at Lissa. "It's just going to be a bunch of women, right?"

"I want you to come." Dea's tone was stern. "It would mean a lot to me."

Lissa looked at her magazine again. *Wow, this isn't awkward at all.*

"Fine," Grayson grumbled.

Lissa lowered the magazine and locked eyes with Dea. *What's going on?*

'Sorry' Dea mouthed and shook her head.

'It's fine' Lissa mouthed back.

"It isn't a lesbian bar," she said out loud. *At least I don't think so,* she added in her head. She didn't say that all the people that were going, except for Dea and Grayson, were queer in some form or other.

When her phone beeped it was a welcome distraction. It was Star.

Can't wait to see you tonight.

Malena and Deirdre have decided to take me shopping. It's torture.

Send help.

Lissa giggled, then looked up to see Dea and Grayson both looking at her. She felt her skin heat up, not just on her cheeks but on her chin and forehead too.

"Is it Star?" Dea pointed a finger into Lissa's stomach.

Lissa shrieked at the tickle and pushed Dea away.

"Maybe." She laughed. "Why?"

"So… you're actually seeing her?" Dea's eyes lit up.

"Wait," Grayson said. "Is this the porn star?"

Instead of answering him, Lissa looked at Dea. "You told him?"

"Well, yeah." Dea started braiding her hair and didn't look at Lissa. "I was worried."

"So, what's it like?" Grayson had stopped playing completely. "What's it like doing it with a porn star?"

"Grayson!" Dea shook her head at him but then turned to Lissa, a crazy smile on her face. "Is it? Have you?" Her eyes went wide. "Oh my God, you have, haven't you?"

Lissa pursed her lips. She didn't want to talk about sex with Grayson there. She sighed and tried to think of a good answer.

"It's…" She licked her lips. Talking about sex with Star felt wrong. It was theirs. Their own. Sharing it felt wrong. "It was okay. It was normal. I don't think her being a porn star has anything to do with it." Lissa didn't mention that Star had actually quit her job.

"It should." Dea pushed on her knee. "But she's coming tonight, right?"

"Right."

Lissa grabbed her phone, tired of the others now.

Dea is asking a bunch of questions about you.

It only took a minute for Star to answer.

You're only giving good answers I hope? ;)

She smiled.

Wouldn't you like to know?
I can't wait for tonight. I miss you.

She couldn't believe her own brazenness. She couldn't remember a single time in her life that she had ever admitted to missing anyone, let alone a *girlfriend*. Her eyes went wide and she looked up at Dea.

"Do you think she thinks she's my girlfriend?"

"Well of course, silly." Dea hugged Lissa's raised knees. "It's a young relationship, but I'm sure that…" Lissa's phone beeped again. "Why don't you ask her?"

"Not over text, what are we? Twelve?" Lissa grabbed her phone again.

I miss you too. I wish we could sneak off and meet beforehand.
Tonight feels so far away.

"She says she misses me." She couldn't keep the happiness out of her voice.

"Aww," Dea said. "She's sweet." Her admission meant so much. Acceptance of Star's place in Lissa's life.

"That she is." Lissa put her phone away. "It's stupid. I saw her just a few days ago and still I miss her so much."

"That's normal, sweetie." Dea threw a glance at Grayson, and for once he looked at her too. It was brief, but it made Lissa a bit hopeful that Grayson liked her sister as much as she liked him. Unlike Lissa and Star, Dea and Grayson were almost always together and had been since kids. It made things different.

A sudden wish to know Star rose within her. To know everything about Star. To have spent year after year with her until they knew each other in and out. Like two rocks in a stream. Shaped after wear and tear.

"I feel like I've gone insane," she said with a laugh and looked at Dea.

"Love will do that to you."

Love? Lissa thought to herself. *What is love?*

CHAPTER TWENTY-FIVE

"You're wearing enough mascara, come on!" Star was standing in the door in Deirdre's apartment, tapping her foot against the welcome mat. Deirdre was taking too long to get ready. And Malena was still in the bathroom. Star wanted to go. It felt like little ants were marching up and down her arms. She wanted to see Lissa.

"Fine, fine." Deirdre came down the stairs, wearing jeans and a shirt. She looked good with mascara and a shaved head. A bit pissed off, but Deirdre was always pissed off. "I'm coming."

"Me too." The bathroom door opened and Malena came out. She was wearing a small black top with long silver necklaces and slacks. She looked good, but the thought only passed briefly through Star's head before Lissa popped back in. She needed to see her now.

"Let's go."

They caught a bus downtown and got out just a block from *The Crying Nightingale,* walking the rest of the way. It was still hinting at daylight, but the shadows were getting longer and the purple sky was covered in fluffy clouds. Little pubs and clubs were open and there were happy people everywhere. Sounds. Smells. It resonated with something inside Star's soul.

By the time they saw Lissa, Dea, and Grayson waiting outside the club, Star felt like she was vibrating with giddy happiness.

*

Star was smiling when they arrived and Lissa hoped it was for her. They greeted each other with a quick peck on the lips, a disapproving look from Deirdre, and a hug from Malena. She turned to her sister.

"Dea, this is Malena and Deirdre. Malena and Deirdre, this is Dea."

"Wow, there's a sister!" Malena took a step forward and grabbed Dea's hand. "You didn't tell me there was a sister!" She winked at Lissa.

"I'm Grayson."

The women all turned around and looked at Grayson, who was standing behind Dea.

"This is Grayson." Dea smiled triumphantly. "My boyfriend."

Lissa and Star shared a look.

If it was news to Grayson, he didn't show it, he just took a hold of Dea's hand and pulled her toward him. He put his arm around her waist and held her close.

"Nice to meet you, Grayson." Malena smiled sweetly. She chuckled.

"Well." Star put her arm around Lissa's waist, "now that introductions have been done, why don't we go in?"

Inside there were people from wall-to-wall, by the bar and on the dancefloor, but Deirdre managed to get them a booth where they squeezed tight together. Star, Lissa, Grayson, Dea, Malena, and Deirdre. How Dea and Malena wound up next to each other, Lissa didn't know, but both looked pleased. Grayson didn't.

But Lissa didn't care, she was too busy looking at Star. And Star was looking at her too, a tender smile playing on her lips. She had done something to her hair, it was darker and spikier. And she seemed to be wearing lipstick. She looked good. Smelled good too, Lissa noticed when she leaned in.

"I want a drink," she whispered in Star's ear. "Will you get me one?" She pressed a kiss to just beneath Star's ear.

They looked at each other, their mouths so close.

"Okay." Instead of kissing her, Star pulled away. "I'm going to get us some drinks."

"I'll come with you," Malena said. She pushed on Deirdre, who was sitting on the edge. "Come on." She winked at Dea. "I'll get you and your boy-toy something too."

They left, leaving the sisters and Grayson alone in the booth.

"I don't like Malena," Grayson grumbled. "Is everyone here a lesbian except for Dea?"

Dea chuckled.

"Who says I'm not a lesbian." She winked, but then she took his hand. "Don't look so worried, Gray. You're my boyfriend, remember?"

"Apparently. And since when?"

"Since tonight." Dea smiled at Lissa.

Lissa chuckled and shook her head. Dea had always been good at getting what she wanted, but this really took the cake.

Star and the others came back, handing out drinks to everyone. Deirdre handed a beer to Grayson with a bored look on her face. Malena handed Dea a pink cocktail with an umbrella and a straw. Star had gotten a beer for herself and placed a yellow concoction in front of Lissa.

"This is called a Lemon Piggy."

Lissa raised an eyebrow.

"I know," Star chuckled. "The name sucks, but my friend made it up, it's sweet and delicious and I think you'll like it. Trust me." She bumped their shoulders together.

Lissa smiled at her. *I trust you.* She leaned forward and took a tentative sip of her drink. It tasted like lemonade but much better. She loved it.

"Thank you, it's good."

A spunky redhead came up to the table, nodded at Star, and put one hand on the table in front of Deirdre. A dark look came over Deirdre's features.

"Deirdre," the woman said.

"Daphne."

The others just stared.

"I think you owe me a dance."

Deirdre crossed her arms in front of her chest, she pursed her lips.

"I'll show you a dance," she muttered.

Daphne smiled. "Creepy. But I like it. Now come on." She reached over, grabbed Deirdre's hand and pulled her up. "See you later, Stars." She winked at Star and then they were gone.

Lissa looked at Star questioningly.

"Don't ask," Star laughed. "Daphne comes and goes. She's good for Deirdre, the only one that can *occasionally* get a smile from her."

"Oh." Lissa didn't know what else to say. She took another sip of her drink.

"I want to dance." Star took her hand. "Come on."

They dived into the crowd together, finding a spot on the floor that was just theirs. Star put her hands on Lissa's waist and pulled her close. They moved together to the music, following the rhythm. At first, Lissa kept her eyes closed. When she opened them, she saw to her amusement Daphne and Deirdre kissing in a corner.

She nudged Star and pointed.

"That didn't take long," Star said close to Lissa's ears. "Usually she holds out for at least one song."

Lissa giggled and looked up again. The kissing couple were gone now.

*

It was close to one o'clock when Dea and Lissa exited the club hand in hand, laughing. After the sisters came Grayson, Star, and Malena.

Dea pulled Lissa to the side. "So... I was wondering." She bit her lip. For Lissa, the gesture was like looking in the mirror. It wasn't often that Dea looked so coy.

"Come on." Lissa nudged her. "What is it?"

"You're sleeping at Star's? So Grayson and I can use your apartment, right?"

Lissa reached for her key. "You're gonna do it in my bed, aren't you?"

"I make no promises." If Dea was blushing, Lissa couldn't tell in the dim light.

"Ugh."

Lissa went over to Star, put her arms around Star's waist, and rested her chin on her shoulder.

"Can I sleep at your place?" she murmured.

"Of course."

Malena walked towards Dea.

"Saying bye so soon?"

"Leave her alone, you idiot." Star grabbed Malena's hand and pulled her into a hug.

To Dea's distress, Malena's hands found their way to Star's ass as she held her close.

"See you soon, yes?" With one last squeeze to Star's ass, Malena finally let go. "You too." She blew a kiss in Lissa's direction.

"Goodnight, Malena." Lissa hoped she didn't sound rude. She just needed to be alone with Star now.

She hugged Dea and Grayson goodbye and then they were finally alone.

CHAPTER TWENTY-SIX

Lissa and Star were almost skipping down the street, hand in hand, blood flowing through their veins, breeze pulling at their clothes and hair. Star couldn't remember ever feeling so alive. And it all boiled down to the woman next to her. *Lissa.* Wonderful, precious, Lissa.

Star knew she was drunk, but she wanted to believe that she would have still thought these things even if she was sober.

"We should get a bus or a taxi." Lissa squeezed her hand.

"Or we walk," Star suggested. "It shouldn't take us more than thirty, thirty-five minutes. And it's so nice out."

Lissa laughed loudly, unrestricted.

"It's feels like it's about to start raining. But okay."

They slowed down, walked together. Block after block.

"Have you slept with Malena lately?" Lissa said when they passed an art store.

Star eyed her.

"Not for a few weeks, no."

"Okay." Lissa shook her head, making her locks bounce. "I was just curious." Her tone didn't show off anything as casual as curiosity.

"I'm not interested anymore." Star bumped their shoulders together. "Come on." She took Lissa's hand again and guided her into her apartment building and into the elevator. As soon as the doors closed, she pounced on her.

*

Star's kiss hit Lissa like a freight train. She kissed Star back frantically, desperately. Hands in hair, hands on hips, teeth on lips. All she knew was that she needed more. More of Star. She felt like she was drowning. She felt skin under her fingernails.

Star groaned and suddenly her hand was down the front of Lissa's pants, touching her everywhere.

"Star," Lissa whimpered and held her arms around Star's neck. "Star, Star, Star."

She vaguely heard a pinging noise in the background.

"Easy," Star murmured in her ear. "Come on, this is our floor."

They entered Star's apartment, Lissa wasn't properly following what was happening, but soon she was undressed and on top of Star's bed, Star sitting on her with her legs on either side of Lissa's waist.

"What did you do to me?" Lissa whispered. "I don't…" She stretched her limbs.

"You feel okay?" Star ran her hands up and down Lissa's arms. "You don't feel like passing out do you?"

"I'm very awake," Lissa struggled to sit up, she wanted to kiss Star, but Star held her down. "What are you doing?" A giggle travelled through her chest.

"I want you at my mercy." Star's smile was teasing, a dangerous sparkle in her eyes. Instead of scaring Lissa, it spurred her on. She called on strength she didn't knew she had, pushed herself upright and put her lips on Star's. The kiss was open and sloppy and absolutely perfect.

She tastes so good. Lissa's head was spinning. She couldn't believe how much she was craving this woman. Needed this woman. Pined for this woman. She hadn't known such feelings were possible. Not for her. For the first time in her life, Lissa felt *real.*

"I want you so much." She leaned her head backwards, slowing their kiss. Her heart beat like a galloping horse. "Do you know that?"

"Of course I know." Star grinned. "I felt how wet you are in the elevator earlier, remember?"

Lissa giggled.

"Would you really have taken me in the elevator?" Their lips were close together.

"Maybe." Star pressed a quick kiss to her lips. "Would that excite you?"

Lissa wrinkled her nose.

"I don't know," she admitted. "I feel like that's a thing I need to think about for a while."

Star's smile gentled. "Do I scare you? Even after all this?"

"I'm not scared of you." Lissa sat back down, creating space between them again. "But sometimes the things you have done scare me."

Star's eyebrows knitted.

"Tell me." Her request was simple, and yet Lissa struggled.

"I once saw a clip of yours." It was only after her lip hurt that Lissa realized she had bit it.

"Don't worry." Star grabbed her hand. "Talk to me. You won't upset me or scare me."

Lissa believed her.

"You hit someone. A woman. You slapped her." Her voice had been reduced to a whisper. "Do you like that? Hurting people during sex?"

*

"Yeah, I do." Star felt calm. "I don't need it to feel pleasure. But I like it." She searched for Lissa's gaze with her own. "But I'd never hurt you, you know that, right? I'd never do anything to you that you don't want." It was important that Lissa knew that. "And just because I've occasionally enjoyed sex like that doesn't mean I need it."

Lissa looked to be deep in thought. She sat with her back against the wall, her chest rising up and down.

Star was burning, wet between her thighs, heart pounding in her chest. For Lissa she would wait. *But as soon as we're done talking, I'm jumping her bones.*

"I want to be your girlfriend." A determined spark appeared in Lissa's eyes.

Star chuckled. "Okay. So be my girlfriend then." She nudged Lissa's knee with her foot.

"So that's settled." Lissa leaned forward. "I like having sex with you, but I'm not ready for... I might never be ready for—" Star put a hand over her mouth.

"Shush, little girl. Don't worry about what you're ready for or what you're not ready for. Let me just take care of you, okay?"

*

Star's voice was just a smooth whisper now and it made Lissa shudder. She didn't fully know what was waiting her, but she knew she wanted it. All of it. She let Star push her into a lying position.

"Is there anything you liked about the video?" Star had gotten back to her position on top of Lissa. But she was sitting at the juncture of Lissa's thighs and was moving in slow rocking movements. It was both soothing and teasing in the same time.

"I liked how indifferent you looked." Lissa was breathing hard. She wanted to grab Star's hips and hold her closer. "Like you didn't care. Almost bored. It made me…" She turned silent, unsure what word to choose.

"That you liked?" Star raised an eyebrow. "I wonder why." She leaned down and nipped at Lissa's lip. "Was it because I showed my power, huh? Like the girl was nothing?"

"I don't know what it was. I just knew I liked it." Lissa's hips rocked under Star's as if by their own accord. Her skin was on fire. "Star, I need you."

Star's laugh was almost cruel.

"Do you now? Mmmm." She grabbed a hold of Lissa's hands and pushed them down into the mattress. "I don't know what to do with you."

"Yes, you do." Lissa arched her back, thankful they were already topless. There was something very sexy about being able to press her nipples up against Star's breasts. "You know exactly what to do with me."

Star laughed again and then in a show of strength, got up on her knees, and flipped Lissa around so that she was on her stomach. She got down on all fours again, holding Lissa trapped with her legs and arms.

"You're my little captive now," she said in a sing-song voice. "Mine to do whatever I want with."

Lissa struggled and noticed that she had some wiggle room, but not a lot, and goose bumps formed on her arms.

"If you tell me 'no' or 'let go' I'll stop, okay?" Star waited until Lissa nodded. "Good girl. Now let's see if we can take your pants off." A hand snaked itself to Lissa's front and undid her buttons and pulled down her zipper. Within minutes, Lissa's pants were off. A moment later, Star's.

Their bodies were completely aligned, Star's front to Lissa's back. Lissa's body was overloading, the sheet cool against her nipples and stomach, Star so hot against her back.

"Mmm, all for me." Star had reached around her front again and was slipping her fingers through Lissa's wetness.

Lissa groaned. She wanted more.

"Inside." It was the only word she managed to get out. It was the only word her brain was screaming. She felt empty. Pulsing. And for once she knew exactly what she needed.

Luckily, Star knew that too. She dove forward and entered her with one finger, to go out and return with two. It was a stretch, but the moment of pain was quickly replaced by pleasure. Lissa dug her hips into the mattress, wanting Star to go harder.

"You feel so good." Star's words were forced. Gritted. As if said with said with great difficulty.

You too. Lissa hoped that Star knew how much this meant to her because at the moment she couldn't get her words out. Something was building at the core of her, sparks struck by Star's fingers.

When Star all of a sudden added a third finger, lighting struck inside Lissa. Her muscles clenched and her whole body tensed up. *Star. Oh, Star.*

She came down from her high a second later, shuddering and trembling.

"Oh, Star."

Star's breath was coming out in short bursts, and her heart was pounding so hard Lissa could feel it through her back.

"Are you okay?"

"I will be." Star removed her hand and instead put her hands on either side of Lissa. She started moving against Lissa, rubbing herself against Lissa's ass.

"You feel so so good," her voice was different. Smoother.

"I do?" Lissa tried to tense her muscles to give Star something firmer to rub against.

"Yes." Star groaned. "You'd feel so much better if I was fucking you with my cock."

A thrill went through Lissa, she didn't know what to answer; she wanted Star to keep talking.

"Yeah?"

"Oh, yes." Star bit down on her shoulders and then licked the mark she had left. Lissa whimpered.

"I bet you'd feel amazing. And you'd love it. Me pushing in and out of you. Filling you up. Claiming you completely."

"Oh, God." Lissa's body was on fire again and she squirmed under Star.

"Hold still." Star commanded. "I'm so... so... close." She groaned and pressed herself even harder against Lissa. "Oh... oh... oh." Her movements stopped and she just held herself close to Lissa. "Gosh I made of mess of you, haven't I?"

Lissa wiggled her ass against Star's wetness.

"I believe you did."

Star fell to her side with a tired groan.

"I haven't come so hard in years, I think." She laughed. "Oh, God."

Lissa got on her side and touched Star's arm.

"That was amazing."

"Yeah?" Star's smile was hopeful, puppy-ish.

She deserved a kiss for that smile. Lissa leaned over and kissed her.

"Okay," she said when she pulled back. She wasn't even embarrassed of her breathlessness.

"Okay?" Star's eyebrows brew down.

"Okay." Lissa pinched her earlobe. "I will go with you. Abroad. But we must be back before October." She laughed at Star's open mouth, surprise and happiness rolling over her face.

"Are you serious?" Star sat up and looked at her.

Lissa sat up too. She nodded. Star's happiness was almost tangible, and it made the insecurity worth it. Like Star had said, they would get to know each other on their trip. Come what may.

Star stood up on her bed and jumped.

"We will be back before October. I promise. Thank you, Lissa. Thank you."

EPILOGUE

Two months later

"What are you doing?"

Lissa realized she had been staring.

"Stargazing." She counted the freckles on Star's arm. There were so many more of them after two months in sunny Portugal. She couldn't believe that she hadn't been home for so long. She felt like a different person. As if she could have sprouted wings and flown them both home on her own accord.

Star placed a kiss between Lissa's eyebrows.

"You're still a bit sunburnt."

"I know." Lissa leaned her head on Star's shoulder. "My shoulders still ache."

"Want to come with me into the restroom?" Star winked. "I could rub some lotion on them and recruit you for the mile-high club. We could go as soon as the plane takes off."

Lissa punched her lightly.

"Like I've said before." She shook her head with a smile. "Completely incorrigible."

"Yes." Star wiggled her eyebrows. "Lucky for me, you like me anyway."

"Well." Lissa threw her arm around Star's waist. "Maybe I'm incorrigible too."

About the Author

Kathy grew up travelling around the world but is now settled with her wife in Sweden. By day she is a primary school teacher, by night, a writer, and with the little spare time she has left she enjoys cooking, playing video games and spending time with her family.

Other Titles Available From Triplicity Publishing

A New Beginning by KD Rye. There's a quietness, an empty space, that surrounds your life after losing someone you love. Autumn lives in that empty space, day after day, following the same routine, in unresolved angst. She doesn't know how to keep her head above water until the arrival of May, a mysterious dream-like girl who just moved in. Autumn finds refuge in their quickly defined friendship. As her mother falls deeper into depression, Autumn doesn't see a way out of her current situation, until May shows her that anything is possible. However, nothing is what it seems and Autumn has to decipher if the relationship she has built with May is real.

I Belong with Her by Domina Alexandra. Tajel Pierce loves the thrill of being a paramedic. Every call she goes on gives her a rush. She makes no time for a personal life. No one can ruin her love for her career. Then there is Arianna Castaldi, who just transferred to her new paramedic position in a whole new state. All she needs is a new start without any distractions. Arianna and Tajel's relationship doesn't start off perfect. Embarrassed of the one night stand Arianna believes she had with Tajel, she wants to pretend they never met and make their relationship strictly business. The only choice they have to keep from strangling each other is to go from denying their feelings to accepting them as they work through intense 911 calls.

Awakened by Fate by Lynn Lawler. Jackie is a woman living life according to her own rules. She's married, but it's the unspoken, open kind. She can have as many female lovers as she likes; she just can't talk about them. After a bizarre encounter turns her world upside down, things slowly begin to change. She finds herself in desperation as she searches for answers. What she discovers is nothing is delivered in a neatly wrapped box. Now that everything has been brought out into the open, she finds she can't run away from her truth anymore. With her new life, comes new responsibilities and a different outcome than what she was expecting. Jackie isn't alone in the story. She meets several new people who help her along her journey.

Nautical Delights by S. L. Gape. Lady Elizabeth Barrington has spent her entire life trying to please her family; constantly opting for a quiet life, she utilises her profession as a doctor to keep out of her families' clutches; bar the annual two-week Caribbean private cruise, where there is simply no budge. Confined to two weeks on board the Iconica super yacht, she intends on keeping her head down and enjoying as much of the holiday as she can, whilst keeping her family at arm's length. Until a crew member catches her eye.

Whispers of the Heart by KA Moll. Days after completing her fellowship in pediatric ophthalmology, thirty-five-year-old Aki Williams travels from her home in Los Angeles to a small town in Illinois, interviewing for a job that she doesn't want. What she does want is to meet her biological sister, Jack Camdon, a sister whom she didn't know existed until she dreamt of her. Three years ago on Sunday, forty-three-year-old professor of archaeology, Carsyn Lyndon, lost her parents and her wife in a tragic accident. Since then, she's suffered from PTSD and loneliness. She's kind-hearted and handsome but dates no one. When she meets Aki at her four-year-old Godson's birthday party, they're incredibly attracted to one another, and those feelings intensify during a family camping trip—a particularly interesting development for Aki since prior to that she'd never considered that she might be a lesbian.

Worlds Apart by S.L. Gape. Hollywood A-lister Heidi Spencer-Brady is everything you'd expect of an Idol. Loved by all, the British Beauty is graceful, talented, humble and so far removed from the 'typical' LA scene. When her husband's infidelity with his new 'leading lady' is leaked, Dawn, Heidi's best friend and manager, goes all out to protect her. She arranges for Heidi to go back to the UK and stay on her cousins farm they had visited as children, much to the disappointment of the animal fearing Heidi.

Castor Valley (Law & Order Series Book 2) by Graysen Morgen. Jessie Henry is torn when she reads about the capture of the Doyle brothers, two young men who were part of her old gang. Unable to let them hang for a crime she's sure they didn't commit, Jessie leaves her wife and the Town of Boone Creek behind, and sets out on a journey back to the one place she thought she'd never see again, *Castor Valley*. Ellie Henry watches the love of her life leave, not knowing if she will ever return. When she gets an odd telegram, nearly a week later, she fears Jessie is in trouble. With no other choice, she goes to the one person who can help her.

Close Enough to Touch by Cade Brogan. Joanna Grey injects the deadly poison into the chamber of the syringe—time after time. She's murdered before and she'll do it again. She's intelligent, educated, and beautiful. Rylee Hayes is a respected homicide detective. Her best friends are her grandparents, her coonhound, and her partner—in that order. Kenzie Bigham is the single mom of a thirteen-year-old, a church secretary, and a woman who's struggled much of her adult life with her own sexuality. Their paths will cross when Rylee's new investigation involves members of Kenzie's congregation. Will Rylee have what it takes to meet the challenge of a serial killer who's proven herself to be a more than worthy opponent?

Fight to the Top by S. L. Gape. Georgia is a forty year old, single, Area Director from Manchester, UK who is all work and definitely no play. Having no time to socialise or spend time with her family she prides herself on being fit and well-polished. Erika is an Area Director for the same company, but in the United States. Whilst she is concentrating so heavily on the promotion she has been fighting for, she's starting to feel like her life outside of work is falling apart. The two women are exceptionally different, and worlds apart. Both of their lives are turned upside down when their jobs are snatched from under their noses, and they are suddenly faced with being thrown together by their bosses for one last major project...in Texas.

***Boone Creek (Law & Order Series book 1*)** by Graysen Morgen. Jessie Henry is looking for a new life. She's unknown in the town of Boone Creek when she arrives, and wants to keep it that way. When she's offered the job of Town Marshal, she takes it, believing that protecting others and upholding the law is the penance for her past. Ellie Fray is a widowed, shopkeeper. She generally keeps to herself, but the mysterious new Town Marshal both intrigues and infuriates her. She believes the last thing the town needs is someone stirring up trouble with the outlaws who have taken over.

Witness by Joan L. Anderson. Becca and Kate have lived together for eight years, and have always spent their vacation in a tropical paradise, lying on a beach. This year, Becca wanted to try something different: a seven day, 65-mile hike in the beautiful Cascade Mountains of Washington state. Their peaceful vacation turns to horror when they stumble upon a brutal murder taking place in the back country.

Too Soon by S.L. Gape. Brooke is a twenty-nine year old detective from Oxford, who has her life pretty much planned out until her boss and partner of nine years, Maria, tells her their relationship is over. When Brooke finds out the truth, that Maria cheated on her with their best friend Paula, she decides to get her life back on track by getting away for six weeks in Anglesey, North Wales. Chloe, a thirty three year old artist and art director, owns a log cabin on Anglesey where she spends each weekend painting and surfing. After returning from a surf, she stumbles upon the somewhat uptight and enigmatic Brooke.

Blue Ice Landing by KA Moll. Coy is a beautiful blonde with a southern accent and a successful practice as a physician assistant. She has a comfortable home, good friends, and a loving family. She's also a widow, carrying a burden of responsibility for her wife's untimely death. Coby is a woman with secrets. She's estranged from her family, a recovering alcoholic, and alone because she's convinced that she's unlovable. When she loses her job as a heavy equipment operator, she'll accept one that'll force her to step way outside her comfort zone. When Coy quits her job to accept a position in Antarctica, her path will cross with Coby's. Their attraction to one another will be immediate, and despite their differences, it won't be long before they fall in love. But for these two, with all their baggage, will love be enough?

Never Quit (Never Series book 2) by Graysen Morgen. Two years after stepping away from the action as a Coast Guard Rescue Swimmer to become an instructor, Finley finds herself in charge of the most difficult class of cadets she's ever faced, while also juggling the taxing demands of having a home life with her partner Nicole, and their fifteen year old daughter. Jordy Ross gave up everything, dropping out of college, and leaving her family behind, to join the Coast Guard and become a rescue swimmer cadet. The extreme training tests her fitness level, pushing her mentally and physically further than she's ever been in her life, but it's the aggressive competition between her and another female cadet that proves to be the most challenging.

For a Moment's Indiscretion by KA Moll. With ten years of marriage under their belt, Zane and Jaina are coasting. The little things they used to do for one another have fallen by the wayside. They've gotten busy with life. They've forgotten to nurture their love and relationship. Even soul mates can stumble on hard times and have marital difficulties. Enter Amelia, a new faculty member in Jaina's building. She's new in town, young, and very pretty. When an argument with Zane causes Jaina to storm out angry, she reaches out to Amelia. Of course, she seizes the opportunity. And for a moment of indiscretion, Jaina could lose everything.

Never Let Go (Never Series book 1) by Graysen Morgen. For Coast Guard Rescue Swimmer, Finley Morris, life is good. She loves her job, is well respected by her peers, and has been given an opportunity to take her career to the next level. The only thing missing is the love of her life, who walked out, taking their daughter with her, seven years earlier. When Finley gets a call from her ex, saying their teenage daughter is coming to spend the summer with her, she's floored. While spending more time with her daughter, whom she doesn't get to see often, and learning to be a full-time parent, Finley quickly realizes she has not, and will never, let go of what is important.

Pursuit by Joan L. Anderson. Claire is a workaholic attorney who flies to Paris to lick her wounds after being dumped by her girlfriend of seventeen years. On the plane she chats with the young woman sitting next to her, and when they land the woman is inexplicably detained in Customs. Claire is surprised when she later runs into the woman in the city. They agree to meet for breakfast the next morning, but when the woman doesn't show up Claire goes to her hotel and makes a horrifying discovery. She soon finds herself ensnared in a web of intrigue and international terrorism, becoming the target of a high stakes game of cat and mouse through the streets of Paris.

Wrecked by Sydney Canyon. To most people, the *Duchess* is a myth formed by old pirates tales, but to Reid Cavanaugh, a Caribbean island bum and one of the best divers and treasure hunters in the world, it's a real, seventeenth century pirate ship—the holy grail of underwater treasure hunting. Reid uses the same cunning tactics she always has before setting out to find the lost ship. However, she is forced to bring her business partner's daughter along as collateral this time because he doesn't trust her. Neither woman is thrilled, but being cooped up on a small dive boat for days, forces them to get know each other quickly.

Arson by Austen Thorne. Madison Drake is a detective for the Stetson Beach Police Department. The last thing she wants to do is show a new detective the ropes, especially when a fire investigation becomes arson to cover up a murder. Madison butts heads with Tara, her trainee, deals with sarcasm from Nic, her ex-girlfriend who is a patrol officer, and finds calm in the chaos of police work with Jamie, her best friend who is the county medical examiner. Arson is the first of many in a series of novella episodes surrounding the fictional Stetson Beach Police Department and Detective Madison Drake.

Change of Heart by KA Moll. Courtney Holloman is a woman at the top of her game. She's successful, wealthy, and a highly sought after Washington lobbyist. She has money, her job, booze, and nothing else. In quiet moments, against her will, her mind drifts back to her days in high school and to all that she gave up. Jack Camdon is a complex woman, and yet not at all. She is also a woman who has never moved beyond the sudden and unexplained departure of her high school sweetheart, her lover, and her soul mate. When circumstances bring Courtney back to town two decades later, their paths will cross. Will it be too late?

***Mommies (Bridal Series book 3)* by Graysen Morgen.** Britton and her wife Daphne have been married for a year and a half and are happy with their life, until Britton's mother hounds her to find out why her sister Bridget hasn't decided to have children yet. This prompts Daphne to bring up the big subject of having kids of their own with Britton. Britton hadn't really thought much about having kids, but her love for Daphne makes her see life and their future together in a whole new way when they decide to become mommies.

***Haunting Love* by K.A. Moll.** Anna Crestwood was raised in the strict beliefs of a religious sect nestled in the foothills of the Smoky Mountains. She's a lesbian with a ton of baggage—fearful, guilty, and alone. Very few things would compel her to leave the familiar. The job offer of a lifetime is one of them. Gabe Garst is a police officer. She's also a powerful medium. Her work with juvenile delinquents and ghosts is all that keeps her going. Inside she's dead, certain that her capacity to love is buried six feet under. Anna and Gabe's paths cross. Their attraction is immediate, but they hold back until all hope seems lost.

***Rapture & Rogue* by Sydney Canyon.** Taren Rauley is happy and in a good relationship, until the one person she thought she'd never see again comes back into her life. She struggles to keep the past from colliding with the present as old feelings she thought were dead and gone, begin to haunt her. In college, Gianna Revisi was a mastermind, ring-leading, crime boss. Now, she has a great life and spends her time running Rapture and Rogue, the two establishments she built from the ground up. The last person she ever expects to see walk into one of them, is the girl who walked out on her, breaking her heart five years ago.

Second Chance by Sydney Canyon. After an attack on her convoy, Marine Corps Staff Sergeant, Darien Hollister, must learn to live without her sight. When an experimental procedure allows her to see again, Darien is torn, knowing someone had to die in order for this to happen.

She embarks on a journey to personally thank the donor's family, but is too stunned to tell them the truth. Mixed emotions stir inside of her as she slowly gets to the know the people that feel like so much more than strangers to her. When the truth finally comes out, Darien walks away, taking the second chance that she's been given to go back to the only life she's ever known, but she's not the only one with a second chance at life.

Meant to Be by Graysen Morgen. Brandt is about to walk down the aisle with her girlfriend, when an unexpected chain of events turns her world upside down, causing her to question the last three years of her life. A chance encounter sparks a mix of rage and excitement that she has never felt before. Summer is living life and following her dreams, all the while, harboring a huge secret that could ruin her career. She believes that some things are better kept in the dark, until she has her third run-in with a woman she had hoped to never see again, and gives into temptation. Brandt and Summer start believing everything happens for a reason as they learn the true meaning of meant to be.

Coming Home by Graysen Morgen. After tragedy derails TJ Abernathy's life, she packs up her three year old son and heads back to Pennsylvania to live with her grandmother on the family farm. TJ picks back up where she left off eight years earlier, tending to the fruit and nut tree orchard, while learning her grandmother's secret trade. Soon, TJ's high school sweetheart and the same girl who broke her heart, comes back into her life, threatening to steal it away once again. As the weeks turn into months and tragedy strikes again, TJ realizes coming home was the best thing she could've ever done.

Special Assignment by Austen Thorne. Secret Service Agent Parker Meeks has her hands full when she gets her new assignment, protecting a Congressman's teenage daughter, who has had threats made on her life and been whisked away to a Christian boarding school under an alias to finish out her senior year. Parker is fine with the assignment, until she finds out she has to go undercover as a Canon Priest. The last thing Parker expects to find is a beautiful, art history teacher, who is intrigued by her in more ways than one.

Miracle at Christmas by Sydney Canyon. A Modern Twist on the Classic Scrooge Story. Dylan is a power-hungry lawyer who pushed away everything good in her life to become the best defense attorney in the, often winning the worst cases and keeping anyone with enough money out of jail. She's visited on Christmas Eve by her deceased law partner, who threatens her with a life in hell like his own, if she doesn't change her path. During the course of the night, she is taken on a journey through her past, present, and future with three very different spirits.

Bella Vita by Sydney Canyon. Brady is the First Officer of the crew on the Bella Vita, a luxury charter yacht in the Caribbean. She enjoys the laidback island lifestyle, and is accustomed to high profile guests, but when a U.S. Senator charters the yacht as a gift to his beautiful twin daughters who have just graduated from college and a few of their friends, she literally has her hands full.

Brides (Bridal Series book 2) by Graysen Morgen. Britton Prescott is dating the love of her life, Daphne Attwood, after a few tumultuous events that happened to unravel at her sister's wedding reception, seven months earlier. She's happy with the way things are, but immense pressure from her family and friends to take the next step, nearly sends her back to the single life. The idea of a long engagement and simple wedding are thrown out the window, as both families take over, rushing Britton and Daphne to the altar in a matter of weeks.

Cypress Lake by Graysen Morgen. The small town of Cypress Lake is rocked when one murder after another happens. Dani Ricketts, the Chief Deputy for the Cypress Lake Sheriff's Office, realizes the murders are linked. She's surprised when the girl that broke her heart in high school has not only returned home, but she's also Dani's only suspect. Kristen Malone has come back to Cypress Lake to put the past behind her so that she can move on with her life. Seeing Dani Ricketts again throws her off-guard, nearly derailing her plans to finally rid herself and her family of Cypress Lake.

Crashing Waves by Graysen Morgen. After a tragic accident, Pro Surfer, Rory Eden, spends her days hiding in the surf and snowboard manufacturing company that she built from the ground up, while living her life as a shell of the person that she once was. Rory's world is turned upside when a young surfer pursues her, asking for the one thing she can't do. Adler Troy and Dr. Cason Macauley from Graysen Morgen's bestselling novel: *Falling Snow*, make an appearance in this romantic adventure about life, love, and letting go.

Bridesmaid of Honor (Bridal Series book 1) by Graysen Morgen. Britton Prescott's best friend is getting married and she's the maid of honor. As if that isn't enough to deal with, Britton's sister announces she's getting married in the same month and her maid of honor is her best friend Daphne, the same woman who has tormented Britton for years. Britton has to suck it up and play nice, instead of scratching her eyes out, because she and Daphne are in both weddings. Everyone is counting on them to behave like adults.

Falling Snow by Graysen Morgen. Dr. Cason Macauley, a high-speed trauma surgeon from Denver meets Adler Troy, a professional snowboarder and sparks fly. The last thing Cason wants is a relationship and Adler doesn't realize what's right in front of her until it's gone, but will it be too late?

Fate vs. Destiny by Graysen Morgen. Logan Greer devotes her life to investigating plane crashes for the National Transportation Safety Board. Brooke McCabe is an investigator with the Federal Aviation Association who literally flies by the seat of her pants. When Logan gets tangled in head games with both women will she choose fate or destiny?

Just Me by Graysen Morgen. Wild child Ian Wiley has to grow up and take the reins of the hundred year old family business when tragedy strikes. Cassidy Harland is a little surprised that she came within an inch of picking up a gorgeous stranger in a bar and is shocked to find out that stranger is the new head of her company.

Love Loss Revenge by Graysen Morgen. Rian Casey is an FBI Agent working the biggest case of her career and madly in love with her girlfriend. Her world is turned upside when tragedy strikes. Heartbroken, she tries to rebuild her life. When she discovers the truth behind what really happened that awful night she decides justice isn't good enough, and vows revenge on everyone involved.

Natural Instinct by Graysen Morgen. Chandler Scott is a Marine Biologist who keeps her private life private. Corey Joslen is intrigued by Chandler from the moment she meets her. Chandler is forced to finally open her life up to Corey. It backfires in Corey's face and sends her running. Will either woman learn to trust her natural instinct?

Secluded Heart by Graysen Morgen. Chase Leery is an overworked cardiac surgeon with a group of best friends that have an opinion and a reason for everything. When she meets a new artist named Remy Sheridan at her best friend's art gallery she is captivated by the reclusive woman. When Chase finds out why Remy is so sheltered will she put her career on the line to help her or is it too difficult to love someone with a secluded heart?

In Love, at War by Graysen Morgen. Charley Hayes is in the Army Air Force and stationed at Ford Island in Pearl Harbor. She is the commanding officer of her own female-only service squadron and doing the one thing she loves most, repairing airplanes. Life is good for Charley, until the day she finds herself falling in love while fighting for her life as her country is thrown haphazardly into World War II. Can she survive being in love and at war?

Fast Pitch by Graysen Morgen. Graham Cahill is a senior in college and the catcher and captain of the softball team. Despite being an all-star pitcher, Bailey Michaels is young and arrogant. Graham and Bailey are forced to get to know each other off the field in order to learn to work together on the field. Will the extra time pay off or will it drive a nail through the team?

Submerged by Graysen Morgen. Assistant District Attorney Layne Carmichael had no idea that the sexy woman she took home from a local bar for a one night stand would turn out to be someone she would be prosecuting months later. Scooter is a Naval Officer on a submarine who changes women like she changes uniforms. When she is accused of a heinous crime she is shocked to see her latest conquest sitting across from her as the prosecuting attorney.

Vow of Solitude by Austen Thorne. Detective Jordan Denali is in a fight for her life against the ghosts from her past and a Serial Killer taunting her with his every move. She lives a life of solitude and plans to keep it that way. When Callie Marceau, a curious Medical Examiner, decides she wants in on the biggest case of her career, as well as, Jordan's life, Jordan is powerless to stop her.

Igniting Temptation by Sydney Canyon. Mackenzie Trotter is the Head of Pediatrics at the local hospital. Her life takes a rather unexpected turn when she meets a flirtatious, beautiful fire fighter. Both women soon discover it doesn't take much to ignite temptation.

One Night by Sydney Canyon. While on a business trip, Caylen Jarrett spends an amazing night with a beautiful stripper. Months later, she is shocked and confused when that same woman re-enters her life. The fact that this stranger could destroy her career doesn't bother her. C.J. is more terrified of the feelings this woman stirs in her. Could she have fallen in love in one night and not even known it?

Fine by Sydney Canyon. Collin Anderson hides behind a façade, pretending everything is fine. Her workaholic wife and best friend are both oblivious as she goes on an emotional journey, battling a potentially hereditary disease that her mother has been diagnosed with. The only person who knows what is really going on, is Collin's doctor. The same doctor, who is an acquaintance that she's always been attracted to, and who has a partner of her own.

Shadow's Eyes by Sydney Canyon. Tyler McCain is the owner of a large ranch that breeds and sells different types of horses. She isn't exactly thrilled when a Hollywood movie producer shows up wanting to film his latest movie on her property. Reegan Delsol is an up and coming actress who has everything going for her when she lands the lead role in a new film, but there one small problem that could blow the entire picture.

Light Reading: A Collection of Novellas by Sydney Canyon. Four of Sydney Canyon's novellas together in one book, including the bestsellers Shadow's Eyes and One Night.

Visit us at www.tri-pub.com